– Liverpool –
MMXXV

MAKE A HOME OF ME

VANESSA SANTOS

dead ink

First published in Great Britain in 2025 by Dead Ink,
an imprint of Cinder House Publishing Limited.

Print ISBN 9781915368829
eBook ISBN 9781915368836

Cover design by Luke Bird / lukebird.co.uk
Typeset by Laura Jones-Rivera / lauraflojo.com
Copy edited by Dan Coxon

Printed and bound in Great Britain by
Bell and Bain Ltd, Glasgow

www.deadinkbooks.com

Supported using public funding by
**ARTS COUNCIL
ENGLAND**

Funded by
UK Government

MIX
Paper | Supporting
responsible forestry
FSC® C018072

MAKE A HOME OF ME

VANESSA SANTOS

dead ink

The lock doesn't exist that could resist absolute violence,
and all locks are an invitation to thieves.
A lock is a psychological threshold.

Gaston Bachelard

as we tried to place that which of ourselves
is something smooth and polished
into the heart of another and the other
knew not what to do
knew not what was being done

Anis Mojgani

Contents

Contents

Table Scraps

The building looked innocuous and plain, low to the ground. Bland grey carpet covered its floors, muting the sound of footsteps. The lighting had been carefully curated, the curtains drawn just so, letting enough of the bright evening sunshine in but keeping enough of it out to maintain a somewhat sombre atmosphere. The windowless room they were brought to stood in stark contrast to that.

The room was large but narrow, the polished hardwood floor catching the occasional reflection from a flickering candle and causing sound to echo slightly. The long table in the dining hall was elegantly set, with a lush centrepiece made of sunflowers and pine cones, as if trying to embody two seasons at once. The plates were delicate white porcelain, with a simple gold trim that glistened in the candlelight. The silverware was polished to perfection. Cloth napkins were tucked into gold rings, carefully placed in the centre of each plate. Crystal glasses caught the light too, and twinkled, giving the ensemble a bejewelled look. The candles were long-stemmed and white, set in simple golden candleholders at regular intervals on the table. They provided enough light to keep the room in shifting shadows, the table a beacon in the middle. No electricity – that had been one of the requests. A candlelit dinner, done right.

The guests milled around nervously, standing far from the table, sticking to the shadowed walls. They, too, were dressed up: long evening gowns, tuxedos, hair curled up in elaborate dos. When they got close enough, every bit of jewellery would shine.

They avoided looking at each other. Their gazes stayed low, roaming cautiously over the table, or finding corners on the other side of the room to focus on. They shifted awkwardly, afraid to break the silence.

A tuxedoed waiter came to meet them, emerging from a door on the far side of the room. He did not come close to them, but stood on the other side of the table, just close enough so the candlelight illuminated his face.

'There are place cards to indicate the seating arrangements. The first course will be served in just a few moments. Please be seated.'

With a small bow, he left.

There were twenty guests. They shuffled uncertainly to the table, finding the neat cards with their names written in gold calligraphy. They exchanged looks, then, as guests who had come together were separated, as each one saw who they'd be next to for the duration of this peculiar, unpleasant evening. At the head of the table, on each side, sat the parents. The mother and father, still married after thirty long years, could barely see each other once seated, the table was so long and the centrepiece so large. They both trembled, bereft of their one source of comfort.

It seemed unspeakably cruel, thought the other guests. This, more than anything else, seemed the cruellest.

They sat in uncomfortable silence for a few heartbeats. Somewhere along the table, someone let out a nervous laugh. Someone coughed. But no one spoke until the door reopened and waiters poured out, arms filled with plates that they set down on the table. Baskets of bread and tiny saucers filled with butter, bottles of chilled wine, jugs of sparkling water. Plates filled with cut vegetables, and little bowls for dips. The waiters set everything down and left, leaving them to serve themselves. As the food was set before them and they were once again left alone, the tension broke slightly. The appetizers before them looked normal, plain, good. They were neither fancy nor weird. They had been half expecting plates of exotic pâtés spread on gourmet crackers. Instead, they had the simplest of things, and they had been left alone, glasses and plates to fill or leave empty as they pleased. This, now, did not seem so bad.

Hesitantly, someone reached for a roll and soon everyone joined in, warming up to the assembly, recognising faces, growing less nervous. They latched on to any reason to pretend they hadn't been dreading tonight, that they were safe now. Bread was all that was needed to cover them in a false and fleeting sense of security.

'So it's a joke, right?' someone said from one end of the table. 'Or like, I don't know, a metaphor or whatever?'

After a beat there was some nervous laughter. Some trepidation eased out of the room as they pondered this possibility and held on to it as a raft in a storm. If it could only be that, they would all survive the evening.

Joshua's mother, Margaret, was seated at the head of the table closest to the kitchens. She felt exposed there as her eyes welled up amidst the giggles around her. She knew each of the people at the table had loved Joshua intensely, had meant something immense to her son. He would not have invited them otherwise. Yet she couldn't help but wish them away, despising their ability to find even momentary solace from the grief by hiding behind their discomfort. Nothing could mask her grief, nothing eased it, certainly not while sitting at that table with all its horrifying implications. How could they laugh, how could they relax, how could they sit there and butter their rolls, dip their broccoli stems into the garlic sauce and lick their lips with enjoyment?

She looked across the table at her husband, but his head was bent and she couldn't see, with all that was in the way, whether he was eating or not, whether it was hunger or despair that turned his gaze downward. She sat stiffly, while around her people nibbled on their appetizers and drank their wine. Some of Joshua's friends were downing it quickly, in a rush to numb themselves to the reality of the evening, no doubt. It loosened everyone, it seemed, the food, the drink. Further down the table someone shared a tale of Joshua wreaking havoc in class; Margaret was too far away to properly hear it, but as the sounds of the subdued conversation drifted up to her in snatches, it seemed to her like a song she recognised even though it was being played too quietly in a different room.

For her, the evening dithered between a surreal horror film and a strange dream she would surely wake up from. Part of her would be forever stuck in the moment they heard the news. Her life had never lost the shape of that day, of the inoperable brain tumour sucking her son's lifeforce away. She had fought him when he refused treatment, but had she fought him hard enough? It seemed heartbreaking to her now, sitting at that table, awaiting a grotesque feast, that he had spent his last few months, the last of his strength, planning.

Martha, sitting close to Margaret, pretended not to notice her not eating and deliberately not making eye contact with anyone. She looked down at her own buttered roll, half eaten on her plate. Guilt curdled in her stomach, but around her everyone else seemed to be eating. Mark and Sayid were both talking about a time when Joshua persuaded the entire class to unite in mutiny. They talked over each other in their excitement to tell the story – Martha could feel the edge to their words, the need to fill the silence with sound, the need to reminisce, remember, cling to Joshua in healthy ways. She was trying to do something similar, inside. Eat her roll, smile at the stories, look sombre but not on the edge of falling apart.

Martha was on the edge of falling apart. She had loved Joshua, with the kind of passion you had to keep hidden, so large it was embarrassing. She had never told him, which now seemed like both the greatest loss and the greatest blessing, though they had made out a few times, at parties, in darkly lit hallways mostly. In the mornings Joshua always acted like nothing had happened, so she had kept her feelings under lock and key. Sometimes they kissed and her hands curled in his hair of their own accord, with such vigour she feared he could read in the touch the depth of her yearning, the desperate edge to her desire. If he did, he never gave any indication. Now he was gone and Martha sat in an ill-fitting black dress trying to blend in with the rest of the crowd. He had cared for her enough to invite her here – the most exclusive party of them all, one could say. That would have to be enough, it would have to be enough forever.

Patrick, sitting across from Martha, fidgeted with his tie. He did not feel privileged to be here – he felt like an imposter, annoyed to be sitting among these people he didn't know. For years he had worked beside Joshua every summer, scooping endless amounts of ice cream at the harbour parlour, trading jokes and sharing a blunt after shifts. Their worlds had never merged beyond that. He had never met his parents or his other friends. Once, when they hadn't, miraculously, shared a shift, Joshua had brought a girl to the parlour, fist-bumping Patrick over the counter, one arm draped over a date he didn't bother to introduce. Patrick had given them free ice cream, drowning their sundaes in chocolate sauce and mini marshmallows. Joshua had looked unquestionably thankful, but he only extended his hand over the counter for another fist bump and neither of them had spoken of it again.

They were superficial friends at best, he felt. When he had gotten the bizarre invitation, in Joshua's own handwriting, it had taken him off guard. He had debated for a while how to get out of it. Would it be disrespectful to do so? Could he attend the service but not the disturbing after-party? In the end he came mostly out of a sense of obligation, and he regretted it almost immediately. Seeing Mrs Marley's grief, in particular, made him unbelievably uncomfortable. He missed Joshua, and grieved him too, but he did not wish to be surrounded by people who felt his absence as a huge life-changing bulldozer, smashing their lives into bits. He sighed, quietly, to himself, and tried to look solemn instead of slightly nauseous.

Next to him, Roger, Joshua's roommate, heard Patrick sigh and considered placing a hand on his shoulder in comfort. He had not met Patrick previously – only knew his name by reading the nametag on the table – but the grief was so thick in the room, and inside himself, he wanted to reach out and ease some of it. He kept his hands to himself, though, as he watched Patrick shove his plate away, a mostly uneaten roll still sitting on it, the butter spread clumsily, stuck in clumps in places. Roger could understand an uneasy stomach, given the circumstances. He wasn't too excited to dig in either, though others around them seemed to be eating easily, even happily. It seemed alien to him, that ease, but he was thankful for it. It lightened the room a bit, made it possible to forget, for the smallest fractions of time, why they were there.

And, really, while Roger was here he did not have to be in his dorm room, staring at the empty bed across from his. He had spent countless nights there alone, when Joshua had been visiting his family or spending the night with a girl, or was just out so late he didn't come home until long after the sun had risen. He had never minded being alone, of course. Had enjoyed it, sometimes, the quietude. He loved Joshua, truly loved him, considered himself one of the lucky ones who bonded for life with his roommate. He had known they would be friends forever, had known Joshua would be the best man at his wedding. Yet now, all there was instead was his yawning absence. What he feared was to go home and see his ghost, stalking the room they had once shared. He hadn't been able to sleep properly since hearing the news, terrified that if he closed his eyes, it would only be to wake with a pressing weight on his chest, to find his roommate looking down at him, eyes glowing in the darkness. He'd never given ghosts much thought before, would have told you he didn't believe in them. He could not explain why this fear had taken over his life, but it had, and, just in case, he made sure to keep his eyes mostly glued to his plate. Still, he could sense shadows lurking against the walls, made murkier by the candlelight.

By the time the waiters returned and removed the remains of the appetizers, Lucy was ready to go home. They brought out the main course and she watched as silence, thick and oppressive, filled the room. The slabs of meat on each plate before them looked normal, like roast beef, or maybe steak. Lucy couldn't really tell since she had not eaten any meat since she was five. That she had agreed to make this exception for Joshua spoke volumes of how much she cared for him. The meat lay next to roasted potatoes and a small serving of green beans. The smell wafting up to her was actually inviting, infused with garlic and herbs she couldn't identify. From the corner of her eye she saw Aunt Margaret put a hand to her mouth, as though to stop a sob, or maybe to stop a wave of nausea. Lucy wondered whether she would bolt or manage to force herself to sit through it. She knew there was no way her aunt could take a bite. She thought she might flee from the table, but that would leave her without an audience for her grief. Was it cruel of Joshua to put his mother through this? Lucy wasn't all that sure about cruel, but it was pretty damn funny.

She ignored everyone else at the table, focused on her plate. She closed her eyes for a second and evoked a memory of Joshua. They were eight or nine, playing by the creek behind his house. Lucy had nearly fallen in and Joshua, half a year younger, was so unperturbed by this that he sat right down on the floor and laughed. She had been hurt – not physically, but emotionally – and planned to storm off in a huff, when her foot caught on a loose rock and she did fall in. The creek was small, but still frightening, and as soon as she hit the water she was colder than she'd ever been, clawing at the ground to keep from disappearing under and getting taken off to sea. Joshua's laughter had cut off immediately, and he was beside her so quickly that she worried he was falling in too. But, no, he was pulling her out, with all his might, and together they scrambled their way to safer ground. Lucy had felt tears coming, the rush of adrenaline making her heart race. Joshua put his arms around her and let her cry for as long as she needed to, and when she was done, he had helped her up and held her hand all the way home.

David watched his niece as she closed her eyes. It almost seemed like she was praying, before taking a deep breath and emerging from wherever she had gone to, only to take up her knife and fork, cut into the meat, and take a bite. The table was quiet, everyone having their own inner battle with the meal before them. Lucy was the first to dig in, and, for a moment, the whole room seemed to be holding their breath, watching her. But she said nothing, barely reacted to the food. After her bite of meat, she had a bite of potato, all the while ignoring everyone around her. She ate with a focused intensity, as though it was a sacred ritual she was performing. David supposed it was. He took up his own fork and knife and heard, even all the way across the table, Margaret inhale sharply. But he did not look at her as he, too, ate a mouthful.

He loved his wife, truly. After all their years together, he still felt grateful to share life with her, still loved to glance up and see her across the table from him, still treasured her warmth in bed next to him. But, Lord help him, she was making this week a greater trial than it already was. It was as though, by virtue of having given birth to Joshua, his wife believed she alone had the monopoly on grieving him. It was as though David's role had been reduced, diminished to that of a side character, only there to offer Margaret support. Like he hadn't lost a child, too. Like he wasn't a father without a son.

His son, when David finally took that bite, tasted gamey. Chewier than he'd have expected, but well-seasoned. He couldn't help but think that whoever cooked his son had done a good job, and Joshua would've been pleased. Everyone had seemed so shocked by Joshua's decision, Margaret surely had been appalled, but David understood. After the initial shock, it had even amused him a bit. It was just the kind of thing Joshua would do, a final trick. Not a cruel trick, not a prank, but something that would shake everyone up. Margaret thought nobody knew a kid like a mother did, but she had been entirely lost when she heard his final request, had fought to undo it. The terrible fights they'd had, David trying to tell her that it hardly mattered what they wanted or how they felt: this was what Joshua had wanted. She had screamed at him then: how Joshua was twenty, could hardly be counted on to know what he wanted. She had broken down, and his heart had ached for her. He saw her so clearly, and it hurt him, too, to see the woman he loved be forced to live with this, a final, unthinkable cruelty on top of the horror she had already suffered. But the father in him spoke louder, in the moment. It made perfect sense to him why Joshua had wished for this. It made perfect sense as he chewed and swallowed and finished his plate.

Lance cleared the plates away, keeping his face impassive. He had to be a fly on the wall, invisible, a mysterious hand bringing in food and taking it away. He would not pretend this wasn't the hardest gig he'd had to do, though. The smells from the kitchen had made him so nauseous he'd had to take a few minutes in the bathroom before this thing started, splashing water on his face and trying not to puke. He was still nauseous as he grabbed plates full of mostly uneaten food, yet he felt indignant, too. The whole evening repulsed him, yet to see that some people had left the meat on their plates untouched infuriated him. Where would they go, these uneaten parts of the deceased? Where have they doomed him to, those who refused to partake in the feast? It seemed to him disrespectful, to come and not eat, after the kid organised all of this. And that, too, niggled at him. How did he know how to set something like this up, who to call? It was like he'd known long before he got sick, what he wanted to do. So young, like that, meticulously planning such a grisly thing. Everything was as he wished, down to the place settings. No one had turned down the invitation.

Plate after plate, Lance carried out the kid's meat, cooked in a variety of ways. He tried to think of it as regular meat,

11

with no particular cannibalistic connotation. The youngsters in the middle, who'd been rowdily sharing stories about the dead kid, had gone quiet, looking a bit green. He hoped they weren't going to spew – if one person started it would, he knew, start a chain reaction that even he might not be immune to. He staunchly refused to look at the boy's mother, now openly weeping over her plate. No one seemed to be comforting her, mostly because everyone seemed to be trying to deal with their own set of complicated emotions. Lance was filled, suddenly and overwhelmingly, with gratitude that he had not been made to sit through something like this, that no one he knew would ever make him partake in a macabre death ritual like this one. He whisked plates away and kept his composure, this gratitude buoying him through the rest of the evening.

In the kitchen, the flurry of activity resembled that of any regular fancy meal, Alistair thought. He did not know how the arrangements had been made, who had stripped the meat from the bones, cut the head from the body, skinned the usable parts, broken a human down into cookable bites. He had not seen any of that, at any rate. Perhaps the chef had been responsible, but Alistair would never ask, only watched him stand over slabs of meat and turn them into food. He had been deliberately paying as little attention as possible, but as the night progressed, he couldn't help but wonder – was the chef tasting, as he went? Was his mouth sampling Joshua before Joshua was parcelled onto plates? Alistair was curious, really, enough to sneak a bite from a plate that returned untouched. It had tasted mostly of garlic and he had not taken a second bite.

He'd been working long hours, taking job after job, his feet hurt permanently from the too-tight shoes he should've replaced ages ago. It paid so little, and the smells of the food being cooked always made him hungrier. This gig had been both different and exactly the same. One day he had gotten a call from his manager saying they had a new event scheduled, a rather unusual one, which had been directly arranged with the chef. There had been a briefing, where the chef had stood next to the kid's lawyer, a tall woman in a pencil skirt suit, and told them of Joshua's request, given everyone a chance to opt out of this assignment. It had been strange and unsettling, yes, but since he would not be involved in the cooking process, he did his best to shut everything out and carry on as though this was just another day in catering.

As he scraped food off the plates, he realised he'd been given no protocol for this. Dispose, as normal? Or save for some kind of ritual? Should he separate the meat or dump everything together? The thought that the family might later burn remains mingled with grilled vegetables almost made him laugh. He'd stayed in the kitchen and not seen any of the guests sitting out there eating, but he wished he was part of it, somehow, could witness it. He wanted to know what the looks on their faces were – not the ones not eating, sending back plates full of untouched food, but those who did eat, who took up knife and fork and sliced into their loved one. He got it, the intimacy thing. You couldn't get any closer to another person than this, than consuming them, tasting them, having them inside you.

Outside, Joshua's dog whined. They'd found him sniffing around the building earlier, a torn leash around his neck, and recognised him from the picture in the funeral pamphlet of Joshua with his arm around the dog, both with wide grins on their faces. He was a beautiful Labrador, with golden fur and big sad eyes. No one had quite known what to do with him, not wanting to disrupt the ceremony in the next room. Someone had set out a water dish and the dog had settled down by the kitchen door, as though he could sense the presence of his owner inside.

As Alistair was considering what to do with the leftovers, one of the new members of the kitchen staff grabbed one of the untouched plates and took it out, placed it before the dog.

For a moment the kitchen froze. With the exception of the chef and an assistant – whose backs were turned, bent over a dish on the stovetop – everyone looked out the open door, to the Labrador sitting there, sniffing the plate.

From the dining room came the sound of glass crashing, breaking, followed by loud sobs. The dog hunkered down on the floor and started to eat. He licked the plate clean and reverently waited for more.

Emily

Emily was never part of the deal. I didn't even know about Emily until it was much too late, until I'd passed the point of no return. By then I was in far too deep to let doubts creep in, too invested, hurtling at full speed towards something I could not really recognise but refused to give up. Emily was a sidecar passenger, I'd thought. Nothing more.

I met Ryan on a crisp November morning. He'd just moved to the city from a small town somewhere off the maps, and he was ordering his first cup of fancy overpriced coffee at my favourite coffee shop. He seemed calm and collected, even though he looked momentarily lost, looking at the menu. He picked something and grabbed his cup and would have sauntered out of there just as calmly if he hadn't bumped into me and spilled most of his hot cappuccino over me. It was the first and last time I saw him shocked and discomposed. Clearly unaccustomed to cramped and overcrowded places, he appeared to have miscalculated his surroundings. It seemed to perturb him immensely, as if this had never happened before and this small misstep proved the unreliability of his perception of physical space and thus shifted his view of reality itself.

He had a brilliant smile, an easy laugh. These I discovered later, after the coffee had been mopped up and apologies distributed all around, to me and the waiters and the other people waiting who hadn't even been inconvenienced at all. He insisted on 'making it up to me', but I would've said yes to dinner anyway. Something about the unguarded look of pure surprise from that very first moment made me think he hadn't been surprised ever before, like he was a newly hatched human, complete with wide-eyed wonder at the world. It was barely more than a fleeting moment, but it set the mood for the rest of our relationship – I would always search for that childlike innocence, he would always be too oblivious to it, to anything that had any nuance at all.

We settled into each other like we'd always been together, like we knew how to fit together just so, with perfect ease and comfort. In record time everything felt easy and effortless and right. It wasn't heart-palpitating excitement to be with him, it was instead a small pit of discomfort whenever I wasn't. My house started to feel empty, full of spaces where someone else belonged. Dinner tasted stale without him sitting across the table from me; mornings alone in bed felt cold.

We didn't see each other that often, surely not as often as I would have liked. We both worked hard, long hours that didn't match very well and often extended well into the weekends. It seemed like most of our waking hours were spent working. If there were holes in his life I didn't know about, then I was predisposed not to notice, to gloss over those empty moments. I didn't want all of his time anyway, I just wanted to be slotted next to him as we both navigated life, not to make a new life together but to merge our separate ones like puzzle pieces.

After four months, he asked me to move in with him. We were both too busy, he said. Dating in the city with full-time jobs was hard. He wanted to come home to find me there. And if it was too soon, well, didn't it feel like we'd known each other forever? Didn't it feel like we were past the brand-new phase and were knee-deep in the comfortable zone? What better way to get to know each other, anyway?

His house was the better option, as it was slightly bigger than mine, and more centrally located. We tended to spend more nights there, anyway. The house had a feeling of newness, like he had just arrived and hadn't really bothered settling in fully yet. It made it seem like the perfect new start for us. Everything was new: new kitchen appliances and dining ware, new wooden furniture picked for practicality, brand-new cream couch that sat lonely in front of a TV in an otherwise empty living room. A new house to turn into a home, a new home I could put my own stamp on.

It was only after I said yes that he told me about Emily. He started by asking me not to be mad.

'You have every right to be, of course… I was just afraid, you understand, I didn't want to scare you away, didn't want that to be a factor in how you decided to love me.'

At first, I was too stunned to reply. I didn't tell him that it had to be a factor, that it wasn't just part of who he was but that it was deceitful to try to trick me this way. How could he pretend this was a detail and not a game changer?

Emily, he said, was a sweet child. She was quiet and kept to herself. She wouldn't bother me and would never, ever expect me to be a mother – no one would. I could think of her as a mini housemate.

We spent a week fighting. Or rather, I spent a week fighting with him while he tried to pacify me in any way, always ready with a logical explanation for everything, including why he kept a daughter secret for so long, and reasons why she would be fine with the presence of a stranger in the house – her home. He was appropriately contrite, admitted that despite all his reasoning there was probably a better way to go about things. In the end we set up a dinner so the two of us could meet, before drastic life changes could be made.

Emily was a new acquisition – that's how Ryan phrased it. She had stayed behind with her maternal grandparents when he moved to the city, just until he settled in. She had just arrived, less familiar with the house than I was, and just making what I had thought was a spare bedroom her own. The city made her a little nervous, understandably, since her entire world had always consisted of familiar faces. He hoped that soon I too would become a familiar face in an ocean of strangers, and that, by contrast, she'd associate me with safety and comfort and get used to me more quickly. At the time I did not question this.

So, on a Friday night, three days after Emily arrived in the city, they cooked me dinner. When I got there Ryan made a point of specifying that Emily had been the one to stir the mashed potatoes and toss the salad. Emily herself said nothing – she stood still and watched me with shy dark eyes, her pigtails messy and limp, tiny dustings of flour on her black dress. She was pale and freckled, with dark hair and large round eyes that seemed to have an abnormal intensity to them, probably because she could hold absolutely still for so long. I didn't know many ten-year-olds, but my mind associated children with endless movement, chaotic activity, colour and joy. Emily was withdrawn, so silent and still you could easily forget she was in the room at all. She seemed barely there, like she was trying to fade into the background and disappear. Sometimes it seemed as if she believed that by staying sufficiently immobile, she would stop existing, or turn into a marble statue and forgo silly human things like breathing and eating.

She seemed to resent existence. Whenever she wasn't staring you down, she kept her eyes on the floor. She picked at her food, ate mostly the leafy greens on her plate, nothing too substantial. That first dinner, she didn't utter a single word, not as much as a greeting or a mumbled goodbye. Ryan laughed it off, said she'd grow used to me, promised me she wasn't mute as he ruffled her hair. He seemed unconcerned and at ease, clearly used to her ways, and I got the distinct impression that this was Emily's norm, not a phase or discomfort at a strange new environment or having a stranger thrust upon her. After dinner she exchanged a look with her father, and after his nod she left and went to her new and mostly bare room, softly closing the door behind her. Her bare feet made no sound. I got the eerie, fleeting feeling that I was watching a ghost walk away.

Ryan sensed my unease and did his best to put my mind to rest. He told me about her extensively, how she had always been a quiet child, even when her mother was alive, how she had a hard time making friends because she just didn't seem interested in talking to any of the other children – but also how she seemed perfectly happy this way, and so, after a while, he'd stopped worrying about it. She did well in school, but didn't seem very interested in any particular subject. Nothing seemed to catch her attention – Ryan said her imagination must be infinitely richer than the real world and everything here must seem drab to her.

I asked if he'd ever taken her to see someone, a professional. He seemed confused – what for? He wasn't going to pressure her into being just like every other kid, and he would never make her feel like there was something wrong with her for being different. He said it so casually, with a conviction that came from never having questioned the logic of it, that I couldn't help but agree. As long as she was healthy and happy. It was up to us to try to gauge that happiness, then, since her communication skills seemed to be so lacking. But then again, wasn't the world filled with useless chatter? Perhaps she was wiser than all of us.

I didn't like her, exactly, that first night. There wasn't enough of her to form any kind of strong emotional reaction to, and that in itself made me a little uncomfortable. Yet I was already placing myself in the 'us' field of Emily's caretakers. Ryan's words painted that little colourless girl in a fragile light: she was precious porcelain, the world would try to break her.

I felt like this family had magically fallen into my lap. They were normal enough, but their edges were tinted with naïveté. It was as if they had lived inside a strange little snow globe and had just now ventured out, convinced the world would be just different enough to be new, while familiar enough to be safe.

If at first Emily threw me for a loop and made me question my relationship, when I met her I finally saw it, that glimpse of innocence that had first drawn me to Ryan. It was such an impossible way to be in this world, and they wore it like it was the norm, the way in dreams the strangest of things seem to make the most logical sense, and when you wake up your axis shifts and you feel off-balance for a little while.

They enchanted me, though I didn't fully realise it at the time.

My mother bought me a snow globe when I was a child, a winter wonderland with skating figures, laughing and lost in a Christmas melody, scarves thrown back as the snow twirled all around them. It used to fascinate me, that safe haven, that magical tiny world, so easily shattered but so beautiful in its fragility. The figures inside so oblivious to anything beyond their globe, unaware of any danger.

I moved in a week later.

At first, Emily refused not just to talk to me, but to talk in my presence at all. Not so much in the tantrum-throwing way, just in her own quiet, unassuming way. And so – Ryan had been right – it was easy to forget she was there at all.

Despite having a young child thrust into the picture out of nowhere, moving in with them was as easy as falling in love with Ryan had been. I didn't own too much; packing up and sticking everything in Ryan's car was the work of a couple of days. He made room in his closet, cleared out half the shelves. They didn't have a lot, either – Ryan wasn't a material man, Emily was still living in an empty shell of a room. The day I officially moved in we painted her walls, a pastel faded-out red that she chose herself, the only colour in the whole room. I slowly discovered it wasn't an unfinished room, it was just how she liked things. Sparse, nearly empty. Muted. She kept the blinds in her room always halfway drawn, never fully dark but not allowing the full brightness of the sun in, either. There were a few stuffed animals she paid no attention to, probably gifts from people that were carted over to the city just because something had to be. She had no dolls, no books, no toys. I bought her a full set of crayons that sat unopened for two weeks before she took one out and started doodling on a corner of her wall. I was shocked when I first saw it, but Ryan swooped in to tell me he'd given her permission – in that one corner she had complete artistic freedom. She drew swirls, mostly, like vines climbing the wall. She only used the green crayon, whose tip was soon snubbed down. She drew for a few days, a week at most, then stopped and left the massive pack of crayons alone once more, looking as pristine as when I bought them except for that one half-used forest green one.

On Friday evenings, right after Ryan got home, we ate dinner in the living room and watched kids' movies – cartoons and Disney, silly light stories and heavier ones. She never commented on them, never laughed at the jokes or smiled at the happy endings. She wasn't scared of the monsters perfectly designed to be an acceptable amount of scary for young children. Her eyes were always glued to the screen – I mean she looked at one spot on the TV and didn't move them the whole time, didn't follow the moving cartoons, didn't look away for a second. I watched her out of the corner of my eye, sitting perfectly still, barely blinking, looking but not seeing, eyes absolutely blank. When the movie ended, she got up and went to her room. Sometimes she whispered 'goodnight' as she was leaving, sometimes she didn't speak at all. I often wondered if in her bedroom she did the same thing – sat and stared blankly at the wall.

To say we were a happy little family is to stretch the truth a fair bit, but we coexisted peacefully, for the most part. There were no arguments, no pouting, no passive-aggressive signs of discontent. Emily sailed through life as she always had before I came along, as far as I could tell, and Ryan and I easily fell into each other, with the familiarity of an old married couple. I made him coffee each morning, except when he brought us breakfast in bed on Sunday. We took turns cooking, or cooked together – when we were both overworked, we picked up food, often forgetting that Emily wouldn't be eating that extra-spicy Indian dish we both loved. She faded into the background, as it seemed she wanted. I think sometimes she herself forgot she existed.

It was a smooth transition. There were moments when I felt an inexplicable dread, like my primitive senses suddenly perceived some threat that my eyes couldn't see. Sometimes the house felt entirely alien – I would be walking back to our bedroom after brushing my teeth at night and in the stillness and darkness I felt adrift from the planet, like I had unwittingly been dropped somewhere outside of my own dimension, an unfamiliar jungle. I still got out at the wrong train stop sometimes, and felt a light shiver when I realised I had to go back.

It was only natural. Everything had moved so fast, after all. Despite how comfortable everything felt, the absurdly sudden shift in my life had to leave me a little off centre. How could it not? In less than a year, I had met someone who filled my life in strange new wonderful ways, and soon our lives were so tangled together you couldn't pry them apart – complete with a kid I now collected from school or warmed up dinner for when her father couldn't make it on time. A child, even one as self-sufficient as Emily, is a big commitment, life-changing in ways it's hard to foresee. Emily's stillness was a distraction, it helped weave the illusion that it wasn't a big deal after all. Most of the time, I believed it. But there were moments when I knocked on her door and opened it to call her to dinner and she would fix her eyes on me, such a focused stare that I often forgot what I wanted to say.

A few times, I felt her watching me that way when we were eating or taking a walk or watching TV together. It never happened often enough to bring up with Ryan, or even try to ask her about it. I wanted to maintain our blessed peace, and Emily, in her own strange way, was just trying to get to know me and get used to me. If she memorised my features, perhaps she'd stop feeling the need to look at me that way, and her gaze would drift back down to the floor.

I tried to shake off the occasional sense of unease.

When summer was ending, the air distinctly chillier but the sun still shining brightly, we took a little family trip. We packed our bags and rented a cottage by the sea for the weekend. We wanted to enjoy the last few moments of good weather before winter buried us in coats and scarves.

Emily

The drive was long but pleasant; we were all lost in our own thoughts but excited, too. Talk was sporadic, but the silence didn't feel heavy, and we arrived energised. The cottage was old, clean but not in great condition, clearly in need of repair. Still, it more than suited our needs, with two small bedrooms, one of which faced the sea. We got there late in the evening, and Ryan and I took a stroll along the sand after Emily had gone to bed. The temperature dropped considerably in the evenings, so we were wrapped up in warm sweaters, enjoying the empty beach and the way the wind chopped up the waves. Despite the cold, it was peaceful and pretty.

We took our time, enjoying being alone and far removed from everyone. Night was in full swing when we got back, and only the porch light was on – everything else was dark. It had gotten cold inside, too, and Ryan turned on the heating, going from room to room making sure all was working properly. That's when we realised Emily was missing.

It was a long and harrowing night. We searched the house from top to bottom, and then the closest parts of the beach with a torch we found in the house. After half an hour outside screaming her name, Ryan froze for a moment, staring at the ocean. We rushed back indoors and called the police and the fire department for good measure. In what felt like record time to me, but likely a lifetime to Ryan, the house was bursting at the seams. It seemed like everyone was there. There was more light than I ever thought possible in the middle of the night – giant searchlights that illuminated everything. All the nearby houses were checked; by three a.m., all the closest neighbours were at the house with us or trying to help in whatever way they could. It's not like anyone could sleep amid all the commotion anyway.

They searched the waters.

By the time the sun rose, panic had been worn down by exhaustion and was edging into despair. Soon a news van arrived and tried talking to us. Ryan was so frantic he nearly shoved the cameraman to the ground. The commotion was both overwhelming and confusing. Why, in so short a time, such a large outpouring of concern, such a spectacle? Later we learned that the beach was notorious for kids getting caught in the tides, the ocean reaching its sweeping arms into the land and stealing little ones before they got a chance to scream.

Ryan was, understandably, a little out of sorts. But he still seemed to walk on solid ground. Anxious and upset, and getting madder by the minute, but he didn't seem exactly scared or unsure. They were hectic hours and I didn't get to talk to him or watch him much, it's hard to say how much worth these fleeting impressions carry, except that sometime right before dawn, I found him slumped over a cup of coffee with a blank faraway look on his face, so exactly like the one his daughter always wore that for a moment I imagined he was speaking to her telepathically, that they had both come from an experimental facility, some secret governmental branch hidden in the middle of nowhere that turned people into something else, something like this.

Much like the flash of surprise when I first met him, it was a one-off deal, sides of him that were kept tucked away somewhere hidden and I had only stumbled upon them. Unlike the moment of shock, this one didn't snatch my attention and drag me close – it scared me a little. For the first time since I joined paths with Ryan and his little family, I wondered who they were. Did I ever really know them?

After three days, we returned to the city. We were still in touch with the police and there was still officially 'a search' going on, but we were given to understand that finding her was unlikely, but finding her alive was close to impossible. The general belief was that she'd wandered out and gotten in the water – as to why no one could find her, well, the ocean is wild and unpredictable, isn't it? Every smile they gave us, every resigned shrug, felt fake and forced, but staying was draining so we got in the car and drove back home in silence.

The drive back was twice as long. It was the fact that I couldn't feel Emily's absence that got to me most. Where a hole should be – a vacant back seat that would swell to huge proportions and feel like it took up the whole car – everything felt normal. Emily was already an only-faintly-there ghostly apparition; I couldn't feel her there on the drive to the beach, so I didn't notice her absence on the way back. It sat like a pebble in my stomach, something niggling in the back of my head that I couldn't pinpoint, but it wasn't until we were halfway home that I realised it was the lack of the lacking that I was noticing and finding so unsettling.

Ryan drove quietly and seriously. A part of me worried slightly that he was blaming me, consciously or unconsciously, because my presence in their lives was what led to all of this, and he was with me when she vanished. But almost as if he could sense my unease, he flashed me a tired smile right as we were approaching the city, equal parts reassuring and concerning. What did that smile mean? Was I reading too much into it, was paranoia beginning to warp my brain? A part of me had wanted that smile, that touch of connection between us, but another part of me wondered what kind of parent Ryan was, to feel anything but despair when his daughter was missing, presumed dead.

It was late afternoon when we first saw the city skylights, and the sun was starting to set when we reached our apartment building. We were both exhausted, but Ryan looked like he was about to pass out on the street. We dragged ourselves up the stairs, lugging the bags behind us. For a moment, neither of us could find the front door key, though we each had one. He finally dug his out from one of the bags, and once we crossed the threshold we dropped everything right on the floor and collapsed on the couch for a few minutes.

The house was cold, but otherwise felt the same. Ryan closed his eyes and I forced myself to shuffle to the kitchen to make some coffee. The thought of food occurred to me, but I knew neither of us had the appetite, so I settled for turning on the kettle and grabbing our biggest mugs. I was pouring the coffee when I heard the sneeze.

I glanced at Ryan automatically, though it was clearly not him, he did not sneeze that small and daintily. I could see him from the kitchen, head snapping around at the sound, then slowly turning my way, too. When he saw me frozen and staring back at him, he all but lunged up from the couch. I didn't follow him. I knew that sneeze, and it scared the living daylights out of me. I was suddenly scared of everything, of both of them, and I did not want to witness their first moments reunited. I was afraid, I think, that they would be strange and too casual, and not filled with the kind of questions that a parent would normally ask a missing child. I didn't want to see it or hear their silence.

So I poured the coffee first, and only then cautiously made my way to Emily's room, where I found Ryan holding her desperately, sobbing, while she stayed still as a statue and let him. She met my eyes over his shoulder and they were as vacant as ever. I had the chilling notion that we hadn't found Emily at all because she'd never gone missing – that she'd been right there with us all along but had finally succeeded in being invisible, had done it so well that we had stopped seeing her for four days straight.

A police officer came round and interviewed her. I wasn't there for it and I didn't ask how it went. Some news reporters called, there was a little bit of buzz for a while, the little girl who walked into the sea and showed up miles away was an interesting story, but we stoically ignored all of it, and eventually it went away. I never asked Emily what happened, though I talked of it with Ryan that night, when he finally crawled into bed past four a.m., after his silent vigil by his daughter's bedside. 'She says she walked,' he whispered to me, and he didn't seem to doubt it.

I didn't press him, just looked at him waiting for more. He shrugged and sighed and told me how tired he was, how the overwhelming joy of having her back was the only thing he cared about just then, there would be time for more questions tomorrow.

But that tomorrow never came. Despite having slept so little, Ryan was up before me, and when I woke I found them both having breakfast, seemingly perfectly relaxed, like nothing had happened at all. For reasons I couldn't quite grasp, I was deeply uncomfortable and dressed quickly for work, though they weren't expecting me in. I needed some distance from that house, and from them, and most of all from Emily's blank stare.

Things went back to normal, eventually, though it seemed like I was the only one who had to adjust – and the only one who couldn't. I tried seeing them as I once had, with a hidden magic, but it no longer fit, I couldn't seem to conjure up the image of innocence anymore, not over my own uneasiness.

Ryan seemed to sense nothing wrong; he slipped right back to where he'd been. Emily, if anything, seemed less there. I tried bringing up the issue again, telling him we should take her to a psychologist, if only to make sure she was okay after the ordeal – if nothing else, she was on her own for days. But Ryan insisted on the narrative that she had stolen one of our sets of keys, walked home, stayed there. No need to discuss how she walked that far, for hours and hours on end, in the middle of the night. No need to discuss the whys. She was back, she was safe, that was enough. He wouldn't hear of anything else. She didn't need to see anyone, and if there was any issue, she would tell us. To appease me, he had a 'talk' with her, which lasted less than five minutes. After asking her if everything was okay and if there was anything at all she'd like to tell us, or someone else, anything she'd like to talk about, he called the matter closed.

It didn't feel closed to me, but I didn't want to push it. After all, I couldn't be sure that it hadn't happened just as Emily claimed. I feared our life was a house of cards that would collapse if you looked at it too closely. So I, too, fell back into pattern, picked up our old routine, and learned to live with a permanent sense of unease.

Then Ryan had to leave the city for work.

It was the first time he was given the opportunity to take on more responsibility at the firm he was working at. It was both a sign they were giving him a chance to move up, and a test. He'd been working there for about a year, and seeing the company give him this kind of trust this early on was incredibly rewarding. He couldn't possibly say no, not when so much was riding on it, when his future there could depend on this trip. He would only be gone for five days.

It was early December then, and extremely cold. Emily was still in school when I dropped Ryan off at the airport. He was excited, and completely confident. He wouldn't understand any concerns I might have about staying alone with Emily, so I didn't bring it up. It wouldn't have made any sense to him – wasn't I, after all, already with Emily on a daily basis, living with her, taking care of her, in some ways exactly like a mother (in other, unspoken ways, not remotely so)? He didn't say 'take care of Emily' right before he left, he didn't mention her at all. We never discussed it; it was a given that Emily and I, we'd be fine on our own. In truth, I think he forgot all about her in the rush to leave and get everything just right for the trip.

When I picked Emily up from school later that day, we drove quietly home. I ordered pizza, and as we stood in the kitchen I told her, 'It's just us girls now, Em!'

I'd never used the nickname before, had never heard anyone else use it. She looked at me unblinking, like I was about as interesting as an ant scurrying in her path. Then she turned her back on me and walked to her room, where she stayed until the pizza arrived. She didn't respond to any of my attempts to start a conversation, answered all my questions about school with monosyllabic stoicism or not at all. When she finished, she asked to be excused and returned to her room, where she stayed in absolute silence.

Tired yet feeling strangely wired, I cleaned up the kitchen and started running a bath. Opening a bottle of wine and grabbing some candles, I turned the bathroom into my own relaxing spa and closed the door to the outside world, both figuratively and literally.

I had just turned the tap off and closed my eyes for a few seconds when I first noticed a gentle rustling noise outside the door. In the sudden silence after shutting off the water, every sound seemed amplified: every drip, my own breath, too loud in the stillness. After a few seconds I settled back down, dismissing whatever I thought I'd heard without even considering it.

But in minutes, it was back. Like someone was sitting right outside the door, leaning against it, and every small shift in position made a small sound against the aged wood. I sat very still for a long moment, straining to hear anything, trying to tell myself it was nothing more than random house sounds, the kind you can't hear until all else is quiet. I couldn't help but feel my skin prickling, even when no other sound came – I couldn't help but be suddenly reminded that Emily could stand so utterly still you'd trip over her if you weren't careful.

'Emily?'

There was no response. I could almost feel her outside the door, a dark hole of inexplicable nothingness – if Emily herself was such an absolute blank, empty of intentions, then what drove her to sit outside the bathroom door while I was in there?

It came to me fast and carried so much relief I immediately sank back down in the bathtub.

'Emily, do you need to use the bathroom?'

No reply, but I wasn't expecting one. Sighing, I climbed out of the tub and wrapped myself in a bathrobe. I was certain I heard scurrying and that she wouldn't be there when I opened the door, and sure enough, the hallway was empty. I knocked on her bedroom door, and when she didn't reply to my call, I opened the door a fraction.

Emily was in bed, covered to the chin in blankets.

'Emily, if you need to use the bathroom you can go now,' I said. My words clashed together and fell out in a rush, like they were trying to trick my head into not noticing that my heart was pounding so loudly in my chest.

She didn't move or reply. I couldn't tell if she was really asleep or feigning it, since her breathing was always slow. It wasn't until I was standing right next to her that it first occurred to me to be scared of another disappearing act. What if Emily decided to walk out of the house and try to walk to her father?

Even though the water was still steaming and my glass of wine still mostly untouched, I couldn't slip back into my calm oasis. I snuggled up on the couch, stole the covers from our bed and camped out there. In the darkness, Emily wouldn't be able to see me if she did need to use the bathroom.

I was awake for hours, and she never came out or made a sound. Eventually I drifted off to sleep in an uncomfortable position that would give me a crick in the neck all the next day.

I dreamt of Ryan that night, that he was at the bottom of a well shouting up to me for help. For some reason, in the way of dreams where logic doesn't always work, I had to climb down a rope ladder to meet him in order to help him up. But when I got there, he smiled and took the ladder from my hands. The water was shallow, hitting me around the knees, but Ryan was strong and it didn't take much for him to pull me down and hold me under the water. I heard him say 'I knew you'd come,' right before I woke up, startled and shivering.

Emily was standing right over me, watching me with those wide blank eyes.

She stopped talking altogether. She ceased answering in even the most perfunctory of manners, wouldn't reply no matter what I told her or how much I begged, stood impassive if I screamed – though it would be days before I felt on edge enough to do that.

When I told Ryan about it, and about waking up to find her there, he laughed. The connection was terrible, and he had very little time to spare, so I couldn't give him more than a condensed rundown of the events, certainly not enough to transmit the sense of dread that had crept into the house and settled in like a low fog at our feet. His laughter jarred me, I wanted to shake him. I wanted him to come home. I thought of asking him to, but I couldn't bring myself to do it quite yet. I kept telling myself I was being paranoid, unnecessarily painting ominous colours in a perfectly normal painting. So when he told me that evening that his trip might have to be extended for a few days, I swallowed down panic and told him that was fine, good news even, if it meant all was going well.

'Splendid!' he told me, in such happy tones I could sense his grin from miles away. How many miles, I wasn't sure.

When I brought Emily the phone and asked if she wanted a word with her father, she shook her head at me, without even looking my way.

'I have to run anyway,' he told me, and hung up within seconds. I stood there for another heartbeat, phone in hand, looking down at this child I had somehow gotten stuck with. She was reading a book, or rather, she was holding a book and looking down at it – in the whole time I was there she didn't turn a single page.

I didn't sleep on the couch anymore after that. I locked the apartment up tight and then I hid all the keys under my pillow. That second night, I overslept, unconsciously turned off my alarm clock and went back to sleep so that when I woke light was streaming in, perfectly illuminating that the bedroom door I had shut the previous night was now wide open. On the third night I woke just before the alarm, and Emily was there, at the door. She hadn't crossed the threshold, but she stood just at the doorway, as still and quiet as ever, watching me.

When I tried talking to her, she turned and left.

I called Ryan almost immediately, with shaking hands that could barely punch in the numbers. I didn't account for the time difference and when he picked up his voice was groggy from sleep. He got mad when I explained, dismissed my anxiety entirely. Emily was a child, a sweet and sensitive child, special and different, and for god's sake did I know what time it was?! He hung up the phone before I was done pleading, and I sat right there on the floor and cried.

After that, I started locking my door at night.

Ryan called less often. His trip got extended again. My nerves were so frazzled I didn't think to fight or question it and eventually found that two days had gone by without word from him. When I called him, he acted like everything was normal, and when I asked him when he was coming home he told me 'soon' and rushed off again.

Emily started scratching at my door at night. I'd hear a faint noise in the early hours, and it wasn't until I pressed my ear up against the door that I realised it was small nails, scratching scratching scratching. When I whispered her name the scratching stopped, but I was too scared to open the door until morning. It happened again and again until I stopped getting out of bed at night and hid under the covers whenever I heard the smallest of sounds.

I called a child psychologist, begged for an appointment, went to see her myself when Emily was at school. I sat in her office and explained, near tears, all that had been going on since Ryan left – since I moved in – since I met Emily, the quiet creepy child who now haunted my nightmares. I told her Ryan didn't want her to see a doctor, insisted she was fine, felt almost insulted whenever I brought it up. But Ryan wasn't here, he had left and left me with Emily, and I was reaching my breaking point.

I begged, cried, bribed, and eventually she took pity on me, or saw how close to desperation I was, so she agreed to stop by the house when her other appointments were done.

I was preparing dinner when she arrived. I nearly burst into fresh tears when I saw her at the door, so overwhelmed with gratitude I couldn't talk for a second. I took her to

Emily's room, explaining the nice lady just wanted to have a little talk with her and I'd be right in the kitchen if they needed anything. We'd discussed this beforehand, her seeing Emily alone so she could try to get a sense of her without my presence influencing her behaviour.

I tried to keep busy in the meantime, made a point of making more noise so Emily would know that I was away and not eavesdropping. Grabbing pots and pans, I eventually decided to make some soup, and soon the sound of vegetables being mashed filled the room. I lost track of time. I got so caught up in what I was actually doing that I almost forgot what was happening in the next room over.

It wasn't until I had everything cooking on the pan – the broth simmering and the kitchen around me a mess – that I realised, with a jolt, that it had been quite some time since the psychologist had arrived.

When I went to check on them, though, she was gone. Emily was alone, and her eyes latched on to mine as soon as I opened the door.

'Where's the doctor?' I asked, somehow managing to keep my voice steady and not betray the emotions building up inside me.

'Gone,' she replied softly.

I couldn't understand. She wouldn't leave without talking to me, and she certainly wouldn't leave without at least giving some sign that she was going. But Emily wouldn't say more. When I pressed her, when I lost control and yelled at her, rising panic clawing at my throat, all she would say was 'she left', in an infuriatingly calm manner. I was scared and I could no longer hide it, but Emily never cracked. Emily's world was exactly the same as always, and she watched me as impassively as she had always done. It was hard to associate that face with the scratching at my door late at night, but trying to mash those two images together, trying to picture the blank empty stare while her small pale hands scratched on and on, brought on a chill that I couldn't shake for a very long time.

I went back to the kitchen and paced. I went downstairs, to the front of the building, but of course I saw no one. Her office would be closed by now, and I didn't have her private number. Restless, I returned to the apartment, and did all I could do: finished making the soup and served it. Afterwards, I locked the house, and locked myself in my bedroom once more.

When I phoned the office in the morning, I was told the doctor hadn't arrived yet, even though it was past the time she usually did, and she'd already missed her first few appointments. The receptionist sounded surprised, and a little concerned. No one was picking up at her place, either. I hung up the phone and didn't call back.

When I tried calling Ryan, the call went straight to voice-mail.

I tried my hardest to keep things normal. I dropped Emily off at school, then searched the apartment top to bottom. I'm not sure what I was expecting or what I thought I'd find – the psychologist shoved in a back closet, dead? Emily might be unsettling in many different ways, but she was still a ten-year-old girl. I didn't necessarily think her incapable of murder, but she surely didn't have the strength to overpower an adult.

Emily

I didn't find it alarming at the time to be thinking in those terms, to even contemplate such calamitous possibilities. I was at my wits' end, at the end of the line. I tried reaching Ryan all day and couldn't get hold of him. The thought of spending another night with Emily filled me with dread, though by then I should probably have gotten used to it, particularly since I was safe inside my room, there was no way she could reach me. I tried not to think about what would happen if she did, not once.

That night was the first night I locked her in her bedroom. It had never occurred to me before because it was such a cruel thing, to lock a child in, and what if she needed to use the bathroom in the middle of the night? But wasn't that what I had been experiencing and living with for the past few nights myself?

I stood outside her door for a few minutes right after I turned the key, listening for movement, mildly horrified by the relief I felt. There was nothing once more, and gripping the key in my hand I went to my own bedroom, and though I closed the door, as I always did, I didn't lock it. It took me hours to fall asleep, tossing and turning and watching the door, listening. I had a dreadful feeling that if I fell asleep, the door would be open in the morning, and all semblance of control would be out the window. I would flee then, pack my bags and leave, take my savings and leave the city, and leave Emily to her own fate. She would surely hold her own better than I was clearly able to.

But in the morning the door was closed and everything seemed normal. Emily acted just as abnormally as ever, giving no inclination that anything out of the ordinary was going on. I felt lighter than I had since Ryan left. Here was concrete proof that there was nothing else going on but an extraordinarily disturbed child. I could contain her. I could lock her in.

So I started doing just that. Whenever we were home and she wasn't sharing a meal with me in the kitchen, she was in her room, and I'd sneak by and lock her in. She never complained, never gave any hint that she was bothered by anything. So, on the weekend, I took a day off – disconnecting the phone line was easy, as was locking up the house and making sure no keys were left behind. Then I spent the entire day strolling through the city, cruising the mall and doing some shopping, eating out on my own. I didn't spare her a single thought until I was in the elevator, heading back at the end of the day.

Everything was intact. She hadn't burned down the place or hurt herself in any way. There were no signs that she had eaten. I heaped up a tray with food and took it to her room. She didn't acknowledge me in any way, and I left her to it, locking the door behind me again.

Ryan finally called back that night, just as I was about to get into bed. He apologised, things had snowballed, the company kept demanding more – I can't recall all the excuses he used. I heard the words, but they no longer held any meaning for me. He felt so far away I couldn't remember his face anymore. I couldn't remember ever having loved him, and I held no illusions that he'd be coming back. I barely answered him, but I realised now that Emily had conditioned him to that, to a silent companion, which he took as an agreeable one. I let him ramble on, until he exhausted all his talk and promised to call again tomorrow, promised to come back home soon. I wished him good luck and fell asleep, peacefully.

Emily became less and less of a person. She no longer came to the table if I just called her out for dinner – I had to go and fetch her myself. She ate less than she did before, and she barely looked at me now – when she did, her face was so sunken that her eyes looked wider than ever, infinite pools, full of something I didn't care to identify, let alone explore. It was easier for everyone if I brought her meals to her room.

At first, this improvement took a massive weight off my shoulders. I could finally sleep without being haunted by a living ghost. No more middle-of-the-night spectres outside my door, and no more vacant stares across the table. Her acquiescence to all the changes in her life was a blessing, and a sure sign that nothing I was doing was out of line.

But the initial relief wore off. Once the big worries were out of the way, the rest crept in. I tried not to think of the psychologist, but she lived in the back of my mind, came to me at night. In my nightmares she was dead, a decaying corpse taunting me that soon that would be my fate too. I was too scared to call back, too sure they would tell me she had never returned and no one knew anything about her whereabouts. In my waking hours, I made a conscious effort to not imagine what could've happened in that bedroom, when the two of them had been left alone. Emily was confined and locked in, yes, but not always, and what kind of prison could contain whatever Emily was? It was better to rein in my imagination as much as possible.

Ryan was out of the picture, I was certain of this. His absence had grown so big it evaporated whatever presence he'd had before. He was gone from the house and gone from my heart. I was increasingly convinced our whole relationship had been a ruse, a clever trap to pass on his child to someone else's care, hand her off without too much blame. A neat way to get rid of her without having to fall into any actions that he was too moral to consider. I considered, very briefly, confronting him about this. Ultimately it felt pointless. He would never admit it, and in truth, I didn't blame him for what he'd done. In an alternate universe, I would admire him and his strategy.

Ryan, I was now sure, was scared of Emily, too.

The claustrophobia settled back in, slowly but surely. The balance was delicate, and sure to crack soon – the uneasy fear that I would wake to find Emily standing over me came back. I couldn't stand to look at her anymore, in her bland colours, with her bland mind. She felt like a parasite, just waiting for the chance to pounce and attach herself to a living organism. I didn't know what to do. How to escape.

It was Ryan who saved me, in the end. Hadn't he orchestrated the perfect switch? He slipped out of the picture, and slipped me in. The formula worked wonderfully before, why shouldn't it work again?

Once I had that thought, it wouldn't go away. It pulsed in the back of my mind, insidious. It was as though I suddenly had the answer and just needed to work up the courage to accept it. Emily had, over time, mostly ceased to be human to me. I could conjure little sympathy for her, but I couldn't just walk out on her either. I think it was fear, mostly. Not for her, but of her. That she would follow me, find me, that somehow I would never rid myself of her. There was very little of the rational left driving me forward.

Eventually the idea of a switch became, in my mind, the only viable solution, the only way out of the possibility of being stuck with Emily forever.

I went to the coffee shop where I'd first met Ryan. Not awfully original, but I was just scouting, checking not just the environment around me but my own feelings on it – could I do it? Could I romance someone else and dupe them the way I'd been duped? Could I sleep with someone else for it?

On my very first sip of coffee, I knew the answer was yes. I wanted to be as far away from Emily as humanly possible and there was little I wouldn't consider doing for that. Her image was stuck in my head like a flag, reminding me the whole time that the ends, in this case, more than justified the means. The anxiety building up inside me was so great it briefly occurred to me to just drive by the apartment and set fire to the whole building, damn everything else to hell.

Crazily, that didn't seem final enough. There was no sure way of knowing Emily wouldn't crawl out of that, smoke drifting out behind her. I didn't trust her to even vanish quietly. No, Ryan had been smart, and he had found the best way to go about things. It was all about finding the right person and weaving a web around them, fabricated of whatever illusions they wanted to see – and once they were dead centre, stuck and cocooned in it, you left, carefully exited and let Emily, the big tarantula in the room, sneak up to the unsuspecting victim.

I started stalking up places, carefully combing 'the scene' for someone who wasn't afraid of spiders. The money I spent on coffee alone was extortionate, but it was worth it, I had to tell myself that, I had to have faith that this would work.

I found my mark at the park. He was reading a book, bundled up in winter clothes but clearly unwilling to head inside where it was warm – he was enjoying the outdoors, and the cold alone wasn't about to chase him off. I feigned interest in his book, I smiled prettily. I was surprised at how easy it was, really.

Not mentioning Emily was easier than I thought. I did my best to keep her out of my thoughts when I wasn't home, and I kept her so well secured that it was easier to go out and stay out. I fanned the passion flames, and after two weeks I spent the night with him, at his place. When I got home, Emily was as quiet as she ever was, and asked no questions. Ryan's calls were sporadic at best, dwindling as time went by. She never asked for her father, either. I no longer offered her the phone. I no longer asked any questions of her at all, and she let me be just as much. You could almost say we'd learned to live together, cohabit peacefully.

It took three and a half months to get him fully enthralled. I did a little better than Ryan – I like to think I learned from his mistakes. I mentioned Emily when I knew he wasn't going to walk away from me for it. I said she was my daughter, and that her father wasn't in the picture anymore, and would never return. I told him, carefully, oh so carefully, planting delicate little seeds to quench future suspicions, that she was a delicate child, who didn't like socialising and often preferred not to reply at all.

Emily

I was apologetic to have kept the secret so long, made it seem like I was scared of losing him, like he'd swept me up in emotions and I was terrified that he'd run because I had a daughter, that it wasn't just me. I was justified in this, I told myself, building this narrative; don't men generally run at the thought of kids, especially the ones that aren't theirs but may end up in their paths anyway? I played the silly lamb, the wounded woman who'd been there before, countless times, who was fiercely protective of both her daughter and her heart and had had the latter crushed often because of the former.

I never knew how good an actress I was. Desperation does strange things to you, it seeps into your bloodstream and dilutes everything down to its essence. Somehow I modelled my words and my body language to convey what I needed to convey, and probably because there was real fear behind all my fake emotions, it came across as pure. He saw a vulnerable woman whose heart he'd stolen, and he noticed I was carrying his own with me.

I had him exactly where I wanted.

I didn't get cocky, I was extra cautious. If things had gone wrong before, I could've just started from scratch, begun my search anew and found someone else. But now everything was at stake – once he met Emily, everything could come crumbling down. If he poked too much at it, if he tried too hard to understand her, or us, or asked too many questions, was stricter than I had been in demands to get Emily to see someone, if Emily miraculously talked and talked of Ryan... so many things had the potential to go so horribly wrong. Yet it was a risk that I was going to have to take, no matter who I lured in, and I was so committed to the cause that I was willing to take it. Worst-case scenario, I could spin my story differently, take the truth and wear it as I wanted it, never letting my underlying plans be known. As of yet, I hadn't done anything wrong necessarily, except maybe not call the appropriate authorities when Ryan dumped his child on me. I couldn't really answer the why of that, if I had been asked, but internally I was aware of that same fear, the need to have something final, that could get me out of the scene in a simple manner. I wanted to run, not get drawn in, and Emily was something unnatural, with sides I couldn't begin to conceive.

I didn't talk to Emily before I brought him home. That would be telling her she had power – I wanted her convinced she had none, wanted her blandness and blankness to be the only features of her that prevailed. I simply made dinner and cleaned the house and at seven p.m. prompt opened the door to another man. I acted like I'd told her all about him, that her shyness was what kept her quiet. She acted much the same way she had when she first met me, silent to a fault, eyes downcast, picking at her food. I dismissed her quickly when she was done, as eager for her to get away as she was to go. She'd behaved so well I almost wanted to give her a prize.

But my target was perfectly convinced. Emily fit the picture I painted of her to a T, and he wasn't even remotely suspicious. He accepted her, but he was also not really inter-ested. Children held no appeal for him, putting up with one was a concession to how much he liked me. It was better than I could've hoped for. He didn't look for holes in the plot, he didn't examine Emily closely, or much at all, he knew little about the regular behaviour of ten-year-olds and didn't have a basis for comparison to find Emily abnormal. More to the point, he was anxious to be alone with me, to be with me. When she left the room everyone was relieved, and his eyes might as well have been glued to me.

He spent the night there, as he started spending many others. I discovered an extraordinary trick, that of making my mind perfectly blank, an empty space. I used this trick most times he touched me. Sometimes I couldn't float away so easily, and in those moments I pretended I was just a woman and he was just a man. Often it worked so well I could fool myself for a while. I never thought of Ryan at all.

It was a smoother transition than mine had been, he wasn't dumped into an unfamiliar world but had time to grow accustomed to a strange one. Much like the frog that boils slowly without noticing, he was oblivious to anything out of the ordinary.

I didn't lock Emily's door when he was there, of course, but she didn't come out either. If he spent the night, she stayed in her room. I almost suspected she knew what was happening – I would find her sometimes watching him with the same look with which she had once watched me, seemingly empty of sentience but filled with something else I couldn't name at first. I might have called it malevolence, if I hadn't been trying to justify the child's actions and make them fit with the version of the world I was used to.

But he didn't notice. If he sometimes got an inexplicable chill down his spine out of nowhere, I had but to run my hand down his back and sneak it under his shirt and he'd confuse it with something else, or distract him long enough for him to forget. I was careful and very watchful those first few weeks.

Ryan had stopped calling altogether by then, only sending frazzled, stressed texts now and again, and though the house was still full of his things, I'd gotten rid of everything that was too obviously another man's. I couldn't throw them out, just in case everything still went horribly wrong, so I put them in storage.

He moved in both slowly and quickly. He didn't move all his stuff at once, in one fateful day, just kept gradually spending more and more of his time here. When his tenancy was up it just made sense to make it official.

I felt a little safer with him there, to be honest. Emily was more subdued, and something about having a solid and strong presence next to you every night makes every danger seem smaller. But after the move was final, I was anxious to leave, for different reasons. I kept imagining Ryan barging back in through the front door. I wanted a different kind of safety, the one built from distance. I couldn't wait to wake up in a whole different life, miles and miles away from that kid. I hadn't really been sure whether I wanted kids of my own before; though I had pros and cons, I'd never felt strongly enough about it to fall firmly in either direction. Now my fate was sealed and set in stone; I never wanted to be this close to a young human ever again.

It was a test in patience, that initial period, lulling him into complacency, getting him used to the dynamics of things at the house, and getting him ever increasingly attached to me. I reimagined myself into what he most wanted – I could see glimpses of it, he showed it to me, I only had to follow through with that vision, make it real. Real enough that he would stay and never think of leaving, but never so real that he'd hunt me down desperately when I was gone.

It was a few more months until the opportunity presented itself. My firm was changing hands, and they were letting some people go. I was one of them, and I was giddy with knowing my time had come, that this was my moment to leave.

That very evening I came home and set the scene. Real excitement poured out of me, and it was once again the delicate balance of something true in the lies that made it all so believable, almost tangible. I was so excited he couldn't help but be excited too. I framed it differently, too, so it wasn't just a few days but a series of different travel stops in a variety of locations – it would take almost two weeks. I told him they were still setting down travel plans for our last few stops, so I had no certain date. I was laying the ground for telling him, in two weeks' time, that I couldn't make it back yet. I was counting on Emily acting fast, but I was also counting on being physically far away, too far to be reached or traced. Far enough to keep running if there was need for it.

I asked him, too, or rather propped it up in such a way that it would make him seem like an asshole if he refused but also gave him a chance to do so. I wanted to trap him without making him feel trapped. It had to come slowly, he had to be unaware. It was the only way. He reassured me, helped me pack, told me they would be fine. After all, Emily was just about the easiest kid to take care of.

I didn't say goodbye to her when I left. I told him we'd

already said goodbye when he opened the front door for me, and she didn't emerge from her room to contradict me. I didn't glance around the apartment before I left, I didn't look back.

It wasn't until the plane was in the air that I felt free.

It was the first time in almost two years that I hadn't felt Emily's eyes on my back, tracking me and following me, even when they weren't pointed my way. I was light-headed with it, the absolute immensity of my relief. It wasn't until much later that I sat down and thought some things through, like the fact that in the almost two years I had spent with her, Emily never seemed to change, not even slightly. I never knew her birthday.

Part of me wanted to call Ryan, now that we were both free, but there was a slight part of me that was still scared. I was sure of myself, and my actions, but that small *what if* kept me from picking up the phone, just in case. This was exacerbated by an email I got, shortly after I left, from the child psychologist. She apologised profusely for leaving without saying goodbye, but she'd gotten an urgent call about a family emergency and had been dealing with that personal tragedy since. She made no mention of seeing Emily again, and in fact said she was retiring from the profession alto-gether. I deleted her email without replying.

He made it harder for me than I had for Ryan. It took him longer to pick up on the nuances of Emily, he got madder when I perpetually delayed my return. He was sure, at one point, that I had a lover I was hiding, and he wasn't afraid to throw 'my daughter' in my face, the one he was taking care of, though we both knew she didn't require the regular level of care. He was impatient and pissed off, but it never occurred to me to budge, just as it never occurred to him to call the police or social services or anyone else at all.

Then one night he called me and talked to me in an urgent whisper from the locked bathroom. He'd woken up with her standing right over him, staring down at him, blank stare, not responding. When he got up, crawling to the other side of the bed so he wouldn't be so close to her, she started shuffling towards him. He sounded terrified when he tried to explain the overwhelming sense of fear, the immediate innate response of his body to just run, and how he'd dashed to the bathroom while she kept marching his way. 'She's still out there,' he said, 'scratching at the door.'

I didn't have to phase him out after that – he didn't call again.

Mouthful

Your first introduction to Marina Kostova's art is likely to have been the pair of bronze statues from early in her career, a medium she never returned to once she made the full switch to canvas. The statues, since sold to a private collector for an undisclosed amount, set the art world buzzing, despite their deceptively simple design: a crumpled cage with a door bent open and a key, twice as large as the cage, with the grooves shaped like birds. The pieces, seen together, clearly struck a chord in the public's imagination, putting Marina Kostova firmly on the map, despite her only being twenty at the time.

Kostova's art shifted over time, but it was her key pieces that she was generally most known for before her disappearance. Painted in large-scale canvas with an incredible amount of detail, they conveyed a sense of claustrophobia, a feeling of being locked in. This was achieved through the use of mostly dark colours and by the contrast of quick sharp lines drafted first, which were still deliberately visible under the new, more detailed paint that overlaid it. Regardless of what the paintings evoked in the viewer, the unanimous consensus was that they evoked something.

The last paintings she did (as far as we know) are, of course, her most famous now. A complete departure from her usual fare, they're done almost exclusively in black and red, with dramatic, almost violent, strokes. The monster, depicted over the course of seven canvases, seems about to jump out and devour you. There has been much speculation around the artist herself and the circumstances surrounding both the paintings and her disappearance. Next year, on the tenth anniversary of her disappearance, the first official Marina Kostova biography will be hitting the shelves. It was with an immense sense of responsibility that I started this project, and it was an immense honour to get to write Marina Kostova's story as never seen before in The Monster Within: On the Life and Art of Marina Kostova. *Printed here, ahead of publication, is a select excerpt from her journals, which were found on her front porch and which I had the privilege to read in full when researching. They are a glimpse into a troubled mind and an invaluable look into the last few known days of a treasured artist.*

Friday, June 3rd

The monster was here last night again. I could feel it breathing around the walls of the house. It was soft this time, like a gentle wind. I could smell its breath coming down the chimney, earthy with a touch of iron, like it had been recently drinking a deer's blood. It was not hard to picture it out there, drinking an animal like a party drink.

I was afraid but not afraid at the same time. I am growing used to it. I will paint with red today, I think.

Monday, June 6th

Spent the weekend whiling away the hours. The canvas stays blank, so does the page. Cannot even doodle on the margins. Drank too much tequila pretending Saturday night still meant something and wasn't just another night. The monster has been away a few nights. I think I miss it.

Tuesday, June 7th

Monster returned last night. Felt huge, bigger than normal. Felt like it was hugging the house – the wood groaned as though under pressure, I was afraid it would pop and splinter and leave me homeless and with no protection against the creature outside. Towards morning, before it left, it scratched at the door, like a cat wanting to be let in. I took a half-hour shower in boiling water. Slept a good chunk of the day to compensate for lost sleep at night. Should become nocturnal anyway, considering how often it visits.

But I cannot paint while it's there, so when would I get any work done?

Friday, June 10th

Monster here, nightly. It rattles the shutters. It cannot get me while I'm inside it cannot get me while I'm inside it cannot get me while I'm

Saturday, June 18th

Are the woods creeping closer? I know this is nonsense. I know it's the fact that I live alone in the middle of a forest with a monster for a neighbour. But still, he it makes the wide woods seem so small sometimes, so cramped. I still recall, so well, first seeing this house and knowing I had to live here. It wasn't the house that convinced me, but the light, streaming through the trees, buttery and perfect. I wanted to lounge under that light like a cat. I wanted to capture it on canvas.

Of course, in reality I never use yellow or gold. It feels… tarnished? Like it's going to turn into a cheap gold coating in my hands and start to oxidise, turn my hands green.

Anyway, here I am, in this dreamy place, where I could spend my days wandering the woods and painting and drinking a glass of red wine under the moonlight. But instead I stay indoors and I make sure all my doors are locked and I read books until I feel like I'll stop dreaming in colours soon and start dreaming in words.

It scares me.

Tuesday, June 21st

The heat has become unbearable. Went for a swim in the lake. Had to hike a bit but swam naked and it felt delicious. Remembered Bill and our nights skinny-dipping and kissing under the water.

No monster last night.

Thursday, June 23rd

No monster. Dreamt of keys, again. I was inside a cage made of keys – the floor was keys, the walls were keys, the door was keys. It had no lock.

Saturday, June 25th

No monster for half this week. Sometimes it disappears like this, for a stretch of time. It's like it knows that its return will be all the more frightening. It's like it's playing a game with me and can't let me get too comfortable. It's no fun if I'm not scared, right?

Must take a trip into town next week, get supplies. Have had a craving for a pasta night, spaghetti and meatballs and garlic bread. Perhaps I should try baking something again. It does get tedious out here, without fresh pastries.

Sunday, June 26th

No monster but dreamt of my mother, holding my head down underwater. It was the monster who came and saved me, but only by accidentally stepping on her and squishing her.

Call Mum?

Tuesday, June 28th

Still no monster. It's starting to freak me out. Have not painted in days but did a quick sketch of something I'm calling Grendel. Sharp teeth, furry, evil. How do you draw evil? Anyway, it ended up looking kind of cute. Not at all what I was going for.

Perhaps I should look to the Victorians, or even the Greeks? Who had the best monsters?

Cannot sleep tonight.

Wednesday, June 29th

Have realised not only do I miss the monster, but home no longer feels quite as much like home. It's like something is missing now.

I have also realised how much I love it here. I drove to town and spent a day shopping, stopping at a coffee shop, going to the cinema. It was nice, but essentially unappealing. I didn't feel comfortable until I was deep in the woods again, trees all around.

I have not seen any signs of the monster outside, either. Sometimes he tramples about, isn't as careful. Like when he broke down that tree that only just missed the house. It's almost like he's patrolling the boundaries, a sentinel.

Or maybe one day he'll take the roof off easily and peer inside like it's a doll house.

Saturday, July 2nd

It's been too long. Tomorrow I'll go looking for him.

Reading Jorge Luis Borges and thinking of labyrinths. Surely there's something to that, keys and labyrinths and being stuck somewhere even when the door is open. I think perhaps I'll try painting today.

Sunday, July 3rd

Set out early, while the morning fog was thick. Not sure which direction to go, but just went. Deeper into the woods. Where it was denser, darker. Where there were fewer birds. More dead trees, covered in mushrooms. Eventually I found a cave, tucked into a hill I hadn't know was there. There was such a stillness. But as soon as I approached the cave, the earth trembled slightly. It's in there. It's in there, I knew right away. I could feel it, a large black hole, vortexing by itself inside the cave. There was no breeze, but this sense of an overpowering menace pulsating from that hollow in the earth. It's there and something is wrong with it.

I left. I wasn't about to do any more exploring. The air got easier to breathe the further away from it I was. Came home and started painting, right away. Have only taken a break to drink some water, eat some leftovers. My hands are covered in paint. I missed this feeling.

Thursday, July 7th

For days I have been painting. Images came to me fully formed, in my mind, images I only had to translate with a paintbrush. Nothing looks how I want it to, though. The strokes are too intense, too deliberate, the colours too bright. Nonsense, all of it, no meaning in the paint.

Saturday, July 9th

Drove to town and bought meat, so much meat. The car stank and I was so afraid the meat would spoil quickly in the heat that I drove like a maniac. I took it to the monster.

I imagined it curled up and wasting away in its cave. I dragged the meat there, as much as I could carry in one trip, left it as close to the cave's mouth as I dared. There was a sound again, a slight shake of the land, an injured animal warning you away. I did not tarry.

I wonder if that will anger it, somehow, my meat offering. Perhaps at any moment it will charge through the woods, showing no sign of its illness, and tear the house down, with me in it.

Monday, July 11th

I went back, the meat was gone. Presumably eaten, as I saw no signs of it decaying on the floor. I've seen no signs of other animal life around the cave entrance either, so I assume it must have been the monster. I hiked back, cooked a bunch of steaks and returned to leave them at the same spot. It prefers it cooked, I can tell. I could sense its mood as I approached the cave. It has taken all day, I am tired and dirty but strangely content.

I think I will make it a casserole.

Tuesday, July 12th

It likes casseroles, I think. I did not take into consideration how long it would take me to hike up there, and it was no longer hot by the time I arrived. Maybe I can cover dishes in tea towels and wear mittens, to keep it warm longer.

Friday, July 15th

It likes sweet things the most – apple turnovers, chocolate chip cookies, banana muffins. A few times I have scolded it, like when I heard a snort of disapproval from within when I brought salmon and grilled broccoli instead of buttery croissants, scolded it like a mother scolding a child to eat their vegetables.

It's growing stronger.

Sunday, July 17th

My supplies were running low again, I brought it some store-bought pastries, the kind made in factories and not by someone's loving hands. I sensed it rise the moment I set them down. The earth shook beneath me. It was coming. I turned and ran, not looking back, leaping over branches, falling over a few times over loose rocks and scraping my skin. I ran as though it was following me at full speed, though I could tell by the silence that nothing was behind me. I made it home and locked all the doors and closed all the shutters, as though that would make a difference. I have learned something of its dimensions while feeding it. Enough to know that the walls around me, the flimsy wooden doors, would be as efficient as papier mâché to something that size.

Wednesday, July 20th
Cannot sit still, cannot paint, cannot read. Have driven to town and back countless times. No sign of the monster. The sun is painfully hot, yet I cannot bring myself to go to the lake.

Friday, July 22nd
I made pancakes, so many pancakes, and brought them to it. It was quiet when I arrived, and I poured the syrup over them right there, fresh. I felt it stir, ever so slightly. I walked away calmly, though all of me trembled uncontrollably. I pretended ease and left as though nothing had happened.

Does it even still need me? It's so much stronger now, I can tell.

Saturday, July 23rd
I have seen it. It let me see it, just a glimpse. the equivalent of a hand reaching out eagerly to snatch the cinnamon rolls. It broke a spell, that first sighting. It's still a terrifying monster, don't get me wrong. But nothing is scarier than the thing whose shape you can't see, forming and reforming itself in your imagination.

I have to see the rest of it, I have to see it and set it down on paper.

Tuesday, July 26th

I have seen more of it, glimpses. It's deliberate, I am sure of it. It's not hiding anymore. I don't always leave right away after leaving food. And sometimes I find it waiting for me, like it had sensed me moving through the woods – and when I arrive, there it is, a glimpse of eyes watching me from the darkness of the cave. It feels menacing and comforting all at once.

Vivid dreams, of mouths with keys for teeth, bitten down on me and unlocking all my doors.

Friday, July 29th

It is here. It has returned, it's outside right now. I woke to its rustling outside and felt instantly petrified, as though I had been playing with fire and a spark had escaped me and set everything alight. It scratched at the window shutters in my bedroom, like it knew that's where I was, scratched gently. A cat begging entrance. I stayed still, huddled under blankets, closed my eyes on some silly impulse that if I could not see the danger coming then surely it would never reach me. I waited for the walls to crumble around me.

Nothing has happened, but it still has not left. Perhaps I will be the final meal I feed it.

Saturday, July 30th

It's early morning. The monster is gone. I have survived the night, though I did not get any sleep.

I could not sense anything from it, perhaps I have never been able to and have only imagined it, projecting emotions onto a creature far beyond the confines of human feeling.

Sunday, July 31st

I returned to the cave. I did not bring food, but dragged a small canvas there, and some of my paints. It did not emerge, but I painted the cave, tried to imagine the entrance as an open border, a place of transfer, and transformation.

Perhaps tomorrow I will paint the cave and paint a door at the entrance, and myself, standing next to it, with a key on a chain around my neck.

Monday, August 22nd

I have been back, again and again. It shows itself to me now. At first it was only bits and pieces, like before. But gradually it emerged and sat so still for me I am sure it knows what I was doing, and was giving me permission to paint it.

It's some of my best work yet, I think. It's like I painted a void, a void that's alive. I cannot look at the paintings for any length of time.

Thursday, August 25th

It has started to bring me food. At first small things, berries mostly, some nuts. Then small animals, rodents, birds. I gagged when I first saw them, but it felt almost rude to not partake? Besides, I am afraid to offend it. It's larger than a house, it could crush me with one hand.

Not that I think it ever would.

Monday, August 29th

Yesterday it brought me a whole deer. I had to skin it myself. I cried the whole time, had to rush into the woods to vomit twice. It's an exchange of sorts. I almost feel compelled to sneak to its cage and scratch at the entrance, but it would hardly have the same effect. The whole woods belong to it, it has nothing to fear. It lures me ever closer. I have started to spend some nights out there, on the hard floor, feeling it close all night.

That cave, its cave, the opening is a mouth, I know it will swallow me whole eventually.

Friday, September 2nd

I went home for the last time yesterday. I looked at its walls, its windows, the wisteria having a second blooming over the porch. I paused outside and sketched it, a final scribble with graphite on paper.

It's only a house, but there's something about it – on paper you can see it, the feeling that something's crouched within it, dark and patiently waiting. I did not go in. I tossed the front door key out into the woods, where it will sit rusting until moss covers it.

Editor's note: It's true that there is a well-established local legend about a monster in those woods. The locals refuse to enter the woods and refuse to talk to outsiders. No credible source has ever confirmed the existence of any such creature. There are recurring references to the monster in Marina's journals for years, long before these last few months, though the first journals she kept when she first moved to the house have never been found.

Changes

The train ride had been long and tedious. Outside the weather stayed persistently overcast, dark, hour after long hour, and Claude, when he'd gone to the bar to get them some food, had forgotten, somehow, her intense dislike for butter and brought back scones, heavily slathered in it. She had not wanted to say anything, for he would feel bad about the mistake and it would spoil the start of their holiday, so she picked at the bottom of the scone and told him she wasn't hungry anyway. He had eaten his scone with gusto and covered the table in crumbs.

Once they arrived, Evelyn, muscles sore and on the brink of falling asleep right where she stood, dragged herself along the cobbled stones without paying her surroundings any notice. Claude had seemed high-spirited on the train, doing his utmost to draw her excitement out, but now he, too, was quiet. It was dusk and the day had been so dull and grey that darkness was not so much falling as thickening, expanding to kill the last hints of light. The town was quiet, the sound of the suitcase wheels dragging on the pavement the only thing they could hear. There was no one in sight as they navigated the narrow streets, seemingly twisting themselves deeper into the heart of the small town.

'You do know where we're going, don't you, darling?' Evelyn asked, careful to keep exasperation out of her voice. It was tiredness, more than anything, making her temper short. She longed to take off her shoes and sink into a bath.

'Of course,' he replied, though he frowned at every street sign.

They had chosen their destination without much consideration: it was a small seaside town, unremarkable in every way. It fit their needs for quietude and remoteness, as well as Evelyn's wish to be beside the sea. They hadn't asked anyone for recommendations or advice; in fact, no one knew precisely where they were, only that they had gone, and would be gone for at least a week. Yet after the long journey, which had included many delays and transferring trains a fair few times, neither had much energy to enjoy the quaint little town.

They walked the winding roads until Evelyn's feet, in her small, tight heels, ached. Eventually they did arrive at the inn, nearly hidden among a row of nondescript houses, just as the last of the light was leaking out of the sky. Inside the house was shabby, dark with heavy drapes covering the windows. At the front desk a dour-looking woman stood as if at attention, waiting for them. She smiled when they approached, an incongruous grin plastered on an otherwise flat expression, as though her mouth moved of its own accord, separate from the rest of her face.

'Mr and Mrs Ward,' she said at once, before they had even reached her desk. She only looked at Claude, holding his hand for a moment too long when she handed him the keys. 'Your room is just at the top of the stairs, first door to the left.'

They shared a glance, as bewildered as it was amused, as they made their way upstairs. The corridor was heavily carpeted, and it soon proved to extend into their room as well, a deep maroon that made the place seem darker still. Evelyn opened the drapes immediately, though it was too dark out to see what their view was. Strangely, the streetlamps seemed to be few and far between, none close enough to cast the faintest of light their way.

The room was small and dusty, the furniture a dark wood, the bedspread threadbare and ancient. There was a desk pushed up against the wall and a chair tucked into it, though there was barely enough room to pull it out and use it. Even the window was small, though the drapes suggested otherwise, the fabric heavy and dragging on the floor. It was fully dark out now, but not even eight o'clock. The prospect of settling down for the night was unappealing at best, despite how tired they were.

'Why don't we go out and find a pub, eh?' asked Claude, tone forcefully cheery.

Evelyn sighed, looked at the bed. The overhead light was so dim it barely lit the corners of the small room. It was a cramped, sad space, and yet part of her, possibly the biggest part of her, would still rather take her shoes off and crawl under the sheets. She knew, without needing to look at him, that Claude wanted to go and sit somewhere warm and loud and drink a dram. Her face must have shown some of her exhaustion, some of her yearning for peace and quiet, for he reached for her and placed a gentle kiss on her forehead.

'It'll be nice,' he said, and took her hand.

Leaving their luggage behind, they retreated from the room mere minutes after first entering. The entryway was deserted, no sign of the strange woman that greeted them. No sign, in fact, of anyone else in the whole building. There was a scent to the place, they now noticed, stale and musty. As though the house was preparing to be abandoned, even as people still slept within its walls.

Outside, the sky was a void, so black it looked clear, though there were no visible stars. You had to squint to find the clouds, heavy and camouflaged, promising rain. They had no idea where to go, and with so few lights about, it was hard to navigate. Claude led them roughly the way they'd come, hoping to stumble upon an open pub.

It didn't take long. On a dark road, not far from the inn, was just the place they were looking for: warm light spilling out the windows, a bubble of noise, a fire crackling in the hearth. And people, sitting and chatting and drinking. Claude did not bother to check with Evelyn, didn't give her so much as a look before barging through the door. She followed, hurriedly, managing to catch the door just before it swung shut again. Noise washed over them. The familiar hum of voices made Evelyn realise just how quiet the town had been, how on edge that silence had put her.

Claude was already at the bar, a wide smile on his face, chatting with the bartender. He gestured her closer as he sat on a stool. Traversing the pub to reach him, Evelyn felt as though she was swimming underwater. There was a hush to the voices now, a weight to their gaze upon her. She felt each glance as a sharp stab and had to work hard to keep walking and not let it show. Claude felt miles away, even as she approached him. He was smiling widely, turned away from her once again, seemingly more at ease with this bartender than he'd ever been with anyone in his life. He looked to Evelyn as though he had been sitting upon that stool his whole life. For a strange, stretched-out moment, Evelyn wondered if she had slipped realities and found herself in an unfamiliar place with someone who only somewhat resembled her husband. She watched him – his teeth looking unnaturally white in the soft glow of the lamps, his dark hair curling around his temples, eyes bright with excitement. By the time she reached him, she was unbalanced, adrift.

He glanced at her encouragingly, patted the stool next to him. 'I ordered you a hot toddy,' he said, with a wide grin, 'to warm you up.'

She realised her skin had broken into goose pimples. She did feel cold, despite how warm it was inside. Though they were sitting at the bar and far from the fire, they could feel its heat, padded along the heat of so many bodies crammed together. A group by the window cheered loudly, clinking their glasses together, and Evelyn clenched her fists to keep from flinching.

She looked at Claude, yearning intensely for a reassuring gaze, for him to look at her as he had always done: seeing her, telling her, with his eyes only, how together they were in the world, never truly alone. But he was still chatting with the bartender, and though she was sitting right next to him, she couldn't hear what they were saying. She heard the drone of their voices as if behind a thick glass wall.

The bartender finally looked at her when he set down her hot toddy on the bar in front of her, a quick glance that held, it seemed to Evelyn, an immeasurable amount of contempt. So intense did it feel that she drew back sharply, nearly falling off her stool. Claude reached out a hand to steady her as the bartender finally moved away to tend to other drinkers.

'You alright there, my love?' Claude said, tone light, teasing. He finally looked at her. Evelyn was sure he would know, immediately, from seeing her face, that something was wrong. How could he not? Her confusion and distress must be plain for anyone to see. But his eyes only grazed hers for a moment, an achingly empty moment, before turning to look around the pub.

So casual was his attitude, his demeanour relaxed and happy, that Evelyn was further disoriented. Perhaps there was nothing to this night, this place, this pub, that was unusual or unnatural. It had been a matter of minutes – entering the pub, sitting next to Claude, receiving her drink. Perhaps her perception had been skewed from the beginning and she had been interpreting the entire atmosphere – the whole night – wrong.

Claude sipped his whiskey and looked around. Evelyn tried to calm her racing heart, to tell herself she was panicking for no good reason. The man sitting next to her still felt so far away she couldn't bring herself to touch his shoulder and gently ask him to leave. More than that, he was so at ease here she could not bring herself to take him away. She debated, briefly, excusing herself and walking back alone, but the thought made her feel more wretched than ever.

Changes

Someone sat on the other side of Claude, somehow obscured by Claude enough that Evelyn couldn't see them. He turned towards them, presumably to answer something they had said, and Evelyn could feel it, the shift. Claude's body language changing, as he turned away from her. Another conversation started, droning on outside her reach. She heard a word, stolen, here and there, no more. Claude laughed at something this stranger said, a high laugh, free from self-consciousness.

Evelyn cupped her drink, hoping the warmth of it would seep into her hands, thaw her heart. Her hands, she noticed, were shaking slightly. The bartender returned, joined Claude and the stranger in their conversation. She looked at the group, caught the bartender giving her the side-eye. It was unmistakable now. She wondered, briefly, if Claude had told him something, something about her that had caused such an instant dislike, almost hostility from this stranger. But that was a senseless thought – it had felt stretched and endless, the short walk up to the bar to join Claude, but it had been mere moments, less than a minute. There had been no time for Claude and the bartender to form any kind of intimacy. Yet it was the bartender that was part of the bubble her husband was in, closer to him now than she was. They seemed deep in conversation, as though they had known each other forever, as though they were the best of friends. Claude was turned away, Evelyn could not see his face. Was it still his face, even? Was it still Claude?

She sipped her drink some more, told herself her perception of time was distorting – surely this was nothing but a brief conversation, her husband was in no way abandoning her, merely engaging in some polite small talk with the locals. She glanced around her side of the pub, wondering if this was custom, if someone was about to slide in next to her. It seemed unlikely, at first, then absurd, for the rest of the pub-goers were sneaking glances at her, just as the bartender had. They did it quickly, in what they maybe thought was a furtive manner, but was, instead, blatantly obvious to Evelyn. Their looks held the same as the bartender's: assessment, judgement, contempt. Something she could not name, like a snicker was hiding just behind their eyes. Was it simply because she was an outsider? But then, so was Claude and she saw none of their looks directed at him.

Someone, a lady wearing a dark purple dress that caught Evelyn's attention, got up from her table and headed towards the bar. Her eyes met Evelyn's and in them she saw the same perplexing disdain. Evelyn sipped her drink, mostly to hide her face, just as the woman reached the bar and knocked into her – a slight enough touch to pass as an accident, jostling her drink, which spilled over her hand. The contact was jarring, frightening, but almost welcome in its tangibility. The woman moved past her without saying a word and Evelyn saw she was headed towards the bathroom in the back.

She looked away, turned towards Claude, now determined to catch his attention, tell him she wanted to leave. Within her a hole had opened up, she needed her husband to hold her hand and walk away with her, back to their dark little room where it would be just the two of them. But Claude was no longer sitting next to her. A shiver went up her spine, she was poised on the edge of a cliff, the abyss beneath her feet about to swallow her up.

Changes

She spotted him quickly enough, standing among a group of men, his back still half turned away. She watched as the man closest to him offered him a cigar. Without hesitation, Claude took it. Evelyn watched the man lean forward, light his cigar, watched Claude puff away.

Claude had never, as far as Evelyn knew, touched a cigar. He knew her dislike for them, shared it – had seemed to share it, had seemed to despise them too, for the entirety of their marriage. Evelyn sat and watched a stranger smoke, surrounded by other strangers with an uncommon aversion to her.

Somewhere behind her, a group roared with laughter. Evelyn was unsure whether she could find her way back to the inn on her own. She shivered, eyed the darkness outside, beyond the windows. It was so absolute it seemed as though the world ended at the pub door. She was cold to the bones. She had never felt so alone in all her life.

Claude glanced back, once. Not at her, but around the pub. His eyes caught hers for a moment. There was no hint of recognition. She looked down at her pale shaking hands, sticky from whisky.

Evelyn rose. It might be too dark out, in this town, for her to find her way anywhere. But it was quiet, too. She knew, because all the noise was inside that very room. It might just be quiet enough that she could hear the ocean, the lap of the waves, the inviting scent of seaweed. She was sure she could find it, even in the night.

She looked behind her, before she left, but she could no longer spot Claude amidst the rest. She closed the door gently behind her, but it hardly mattered – no one noticed her leave.

Make a Home of Me

They'd been living there for just under a year when the house started leaving them notes.

It was the youngest child, Lizzie, who first uncovered them, so naturally no one believed it at first. They indulged her, and laughed or spun her a story, but then they walked away and didn't think of it again. After a while they got exasperated and concerned and started warning her about lies and how you shouldn't trick people, even if you're just trying to create a funny story. No one thought too hard about the fact that Lizzie herself couldn't have written them, or could barely understand what they said, for surely this was a prank of sorts cooked up with her sister.

Lizzie didn't understand, and frowned at the grownups, who should hold within them all the wisdom in the world, she thought, but were already starting to fail her.

Slowly, but surely, everyone else started finding them too. In drawers, mostly, but sometimes under carpets, or suddenly on tabletops, or between the pages of whatever book someone just happened to pull off the shelf. It was bizarre, and one evening they had a family meeting about it. Mr Fink looked at the girls before him: his wife, still so radiantly beautiful, even as she sat and wrung her hands worriedly; Janet, impatiently chewing on her bubble gum; and Lizzie, with her golden locks and wide blue eyes, looking exactly like a porcelain doll and sitting just as still.

'Now, girls,' Mr Fink said, eyes flitting from daughter to daughter, before settling on Janet. 'Fess up now. This business with the notes was fun while it lasted, but it's time for it to end.'

It was all a show, of course. It was easier to call everyone here and pretend like it was a mystery, these notes, and ask for whoever was behind them to quit it. It could only be Janet, naturally, as little Lizzie had just started to learn her ABCs and whatever she could manage to write would always be distinctly identifiable as hers. But neither of the parents wanted to outright accuse Janet, conscious of the delicate nature of their relationship. They told themselves it was a rebellious phase, that all kids had them, tried to chuckle at the memories of their own teenage years. But they worried nonetheless, as parents do, and they'd do just about anything to avoid any actual confrontation.

Janet eyed her parents, then her little sister, before huffing out of the room. She understood all of this clearly, but the notes were starting to creep her out and she didn't want to have to admit it, certainly not when no one would believe her.

They tried to ignore them, for a little while longer, but when Janet went to spend a weekend with a friend and her family by the sea, the notes showed up still. In unexpected places, moved there by invisible hands. They searched Janet's room, but found no stash of secret notes; interrogated her sister, but Lizzie didn't even know what 'scheme' meant and nearly burst into tears when Mr Fink shook her in his exasperation to get answers.

The notes got stranger, too. No one could remember what the first ones said anymore, except that they referred to themselves (the note-writer) as the house. But now they were paying attention, and they were decidedly disconcerting. A 'who are you' folded into a fresh bath towel in the bathroom cabinet, a faint 'can you explain time' curled inside Mr Fink's favourite coffee cup, a half-crumpled 'isn't it funny' hidden in Lizzie's pillowcase. No one could make sense of them, but they filled the house, and its inhabitants, with something akin to dread.

The Finks went to the police. They reported the strange notes, how they questioned the girls but had been obligated to set them aside for obvious reasons. They worried someone was stalking them, sneaking into their house, hiding in the shadows to leave them cryptic notes.

The police listened, even did a full sweep of the house, promised to keep an eye on them and left a number, in case they ever saw someone. The officer told the family to be extra careful and extra watchful – keep an eye on the house's surroundings, pay attention when they left the house. Stick together, and never, ever go into the woods alone.

The house was a beautiful one, though part of its beauty lay exactly in the outdoors around it – wild untamed nature that crept up against the house, in vines that had started to climb against one side of it. It was a large house, but old, and not very well maintained. That's how they'd been able to afford it, and in the first few months there had been a steady stream of upkeeps and fixing-up of odds and ends that just didn't quite cut it. 'Quirks,' Mr Fink called them, and smiled at his girls, never once regretting their decision to buy the place.

Everyone felt a kind of vagueness in their worry and fear. They went through the steps mechanically, felt the emotions but couldn't work up a panic. It was muted, each person having this hazy belief that it was someone in the family still playing a prank, with no one in particular in mind and no solid notion of why or even what was happening. They carried on. Notes kept appearing, and though they were always deeply discombobulating, nothing else happened so it was easier to shrug off and get used to it. There was a tension in the house, of course, a sense of waiting for the axe to drop, for the notes to become threatening, someone to finally crawl out of the woods and pay them an unpleasant visit. They became fastidious about checking locks, securing the house at all times, installing sturdier blinds, replacing the locks, making sure everyone felt equally invested in the process of making sure. It nudged them and changed them, shaping them slightly around this fear that didn't taste like fear, this new aspect of their lives that was unusual and perturbing but never kept any of the Finks up at night. They developed these new traits, this new alertness, mutually but silently – they never talked about it anymore, beyond sharing the notes with each other as they appeared.

The notes changed too. Always unpredictable, often nonsensical, they became personal. A note on the fridge saying 'you're almost out of milk', a note resting atop the hood of the car parked in the garage saying 'check your tyres', a note by Janet's backpack saying 'you forgot your homework'. They became, in other words, involved with the Finks' life. This chilling new development was dutifully reported to the police, who returned and searched the house again, grilled every member, took a note for investigation. An older officer spoke to Mr Fink and tried to convince the family to go away for a little while, the police could keep an eye on the house, test the boundaries of this invisible new family member, so to speak.

The family refused to go. Mr Fink ranted about being chased from his property, Janet yelled at her parents about horror movies and impending doom. Mrs Fink became withdrawn, absent, starring into nothing, face smooth and unperturbed. Little Lizzie grew solemn, always serious in front of her family, but quietly crying into her pillow at night.

The house adapted. In the morning, Lizzie started finding drawings in her nightstand, colourful and happy, suns and rainbows and flowers. She chose not to show the others – these were her notes, this was the house comforting her while her family fell further and further away from her. She began whispering to the walls in the evenings, finally finding an outlet for all her fears. The silence didn't feel oppressive or frightening at all, it sounded like the quiet of a friend listening.

The house listened. To Janet sneaking out her bedroom window late at night, to Mr Fink muttering under his breath whenever a new note appeared, to Mrs Fink sitting quietly and alone in her bedroom, wrapped up in blankets, breathing softly, as one who doesn't dare disturb the universe. And to little Lizzie, who cried less and less and learned to trust the presence who comforted her at night.

No one was exactly surprised when Mrs Fink was found. No one except her husband, who had studiously ignored her silences and blank stares, too full of his own words to note the absence of any others. He was the one who found her, in their private bathroom, lying in cold water. It took him longer than it should have to register what he was seeing. The scene had a movie-like quality to it that made it seem unreal: the empty bottle of pills, the congealed pools of blood. The stillness of the room the most obvious sign that no soul lingered here. He managed to keep Lizzie away, but not Janet, who barged in when his throat betrayed him and gave out a hollow scream. There were no notes that day.

Janet withdrew into herself much like her mother before her. Her silences became longer and weightier. Mr Fink sank into his own grief like a stone upon a lake. For two weeks, the house was so quiet you'd be forgiven for thinking it empty, abandoned. Its inhabitants moved upon the world with small, subdued steps. They forgot the notes, all but Lizzie, who still talked to the house at night, leaned against the walls like a child against a mother, awaiting an embrace. But the notes she got she kept to herself, told no one. No one asked her much anyway.

After two weeks, though, there was a new note on the fridge, left just as all the others before it. Janet saw it first, on an annoyingly bright Saturday morning. She called for her dad, standing in the doorway, refusing to take another step forward. The words were legible from there, anyway: *it is better this way.*

The girls had never seen their father so angry. He punched the hallway wall, hard enough to leave a dent there and bloody his knuckles. He would've stepped into the kitchen and torn the note to pieces, if Janet hadn't stopped him, begged him to call the police, show them this note. When they came they brought a detective, a short man whom they called Mr Rhys, who grabbed the note carefully with pincers and placed it inside a plastic bag. He asked them if anyone had touched it, asked them about previous notes, about Mrs Fink's death. Lizzie stumbled half-asleep into the kitchen halfway through this, endured her own set of questions, though gentler ones that she answered from her father's lap with a heavy voice.

'Do you know who's leaving these, Lizzie?' Mr Rhys asked her, his voice level. She had been asked this before, by other policemen, had dutifully shaken her head or shrugged her shoulders. But she knew now, and she could not keep that knowledge from showing on her face. So she said, very simply: 'It's the house.'

'Why would the house think it's better that your mommy is gone?' he asked, after the briefest of pauses.

'Because she was sad all the time and didn't take care of us.'

Mr Rhys left, then. Mr Fink's face was ashen white, and he could not meet Lizzie's eyes. Janet locked herself in her room and didn't come out again until evening. No one asked Lizzie any further questions.

Eventually someone thought to suggest security cameras, installed inside the house. Mr Fink took the idea hard, for how simple and basic it was, for how useful it could have been before. He wasn't sure what he thought of the notes anymore, other than he tried his best not to think of them at all. Nonetheless, the cameras were installed, and reviewed as soon as the next note appeared, underneath a couch pillow. Yet the images showed nothing, no unusual movement, no one even going into the living room until Janet found the note while looking for a lost earing. They were sure it hadn't been there last time they had sat on the couch (when was that?) yet couldn't rule out a note lying unnoticed for a long time, and so dismissed it, and waited for the next note. The next day one appeared in the freezer, stuck to an ice-cream carton, and, again, video footage showed nothing.

Mr Fink, sunken into shock and grief, couldn't think of when he'd last opened the freezer. Could barely remember the last time he'd made food and not just grabbed takeaway. He determined to search the house top to bottom, to find any potentially missed notes. It took an entire day, stretched well into the night. All he found was Lizzie's hidden stash. He knew, right away, that they were not his daughter's creations, even the simplest of drawings. They had a stamp of something else, they told a story when put together.

For the first time in her short life, little Lizzie was afraid of her father. He loomed so large above her, he screamed so loud. When he grabbed her arms, his hands dug into them so hard she started to cry. Janet emerged, pulled her little sister away, startled their father out of his warpath. He backed away from them slowly, eyes wide and lost, looked at them as if he had never seen them before, as if he had just woken up into a nightmare world. He left, but took Lizzie's drawings, didn't even look back when she begged him not to, her little-girl voice breaking down into sobs. Janet held her hand, pulled her along so they could follow their father.

They found him kneeling by the fireplace, trying to coax a fire into life. Lizzie pleaded, though Janet held her back from going to him. Her voice, her tears, so loud for such small lungs, were a symphony echoing in the living room. The fire caught, and roared up, nearly scorched Mr Fink, who fell back. It gave him pause, that fire, but he still threw the stash of papers in, and all three of them stood and watched them burn. When Mr Fink looked up and saw his daughters, standing still and shocked, he felt a tremor inside him, something breaking open. But he was too tired – he watched them leave and curled up by the fire, fell asleep instantly.

Janet was gone by morning. She kissed her sister's tear-streaked face, after she had finally fallen into exhausted sleep. She couldn't bear to actually say goodbye, thought of leaving a note and quickly dismissed the absurd, ironic notion. She took only a backpack full of stuff and never came back for anything else.

Mr Fink hardly seemed to notice. Something had come untethered inside him; he floated through the house, a purposeless ghost. Lizzie knew better than to mention Janet, knew better than to even try talking to her father now. She avoided him, the image of his distorted, enraged face permanently scarred into her mind. She didn't need him, anyway. The house would take care of her.

For a short while, they carried on like this, a half-existence, a silent house. There were a few phone calls before those stopped, as people drifted off into their own lives and left them to their grief. Mr Rhys, the detective, stopped by once more. But there was nothing else to see – no more notes, only a man bent down by loss, and his child staring up at him with sad, unblinking eyes. It didn't surprise him to find the eldest daughter gone. Their home had become infected, getting eaten from the inside by the colossal absence of Mrs Fink, undone by the strange circumstances around it. Neither Lizzie nor Mr Fink told him of the pile of notes and drawings turned to ashes in the fireplace. It wasn't crazy to think, the detective thought, that Janet had somehow orchestrated everything all along, and had left when her mother committed suicide, chased away by the enormous guilt. Mr Rhys left, making a mental note to keep an eye on what was left of the family, to make sure the little one was still being taken care of. The detective got in his car and drove away, and never thought of Lizzie again.

When the first snow fell, Lizzie woke to find her room toasty warm, the radiator set to full blast. Though winter had hunkered down for a while now, Mr Fink was inconsistent with the heating, leaving whole rooms to sit in the cold, forgetting to turn it on at all for days. Lizzie would huddle under her blankets and stare out the window, watching as the glass frosted over.

But that morning there was warmth, and comfort. And a note on her bedside table that said, she could just make out, *good morning*. When she made her way to the kitchen, the table was set for one, a plate heaped with hot pancakes just waiting for her. The house seemed clean, sparkling, for the first time in a long time. Gone was the smell of rotting food left too long in the fridge, the layers of dust collecting over everything, the dirty dishes heaped in the sink. Lizzie ate while watching the snow fall outside, covering the ground. Perhaps in a few hours there would be enough snow for a snowman.

When she walked past her parents' bedroom, the door was shut. She tried the handle, but it was locked. The handle was cold to the touch, and when Lizzie laid her hand against the wood, so was the door. A breeze touched her feet from the gap at the bottom. She shivered, and moved on, drawn by the crackling fire in the living room. There was a colouring book waiting for her on the coffee table, a plate of cookies next to it.

In the spring the ice would thaw. Mr Fink's body would start to decompose and smell. Eventually someone would come – someone would walk past and smell something foul, a distant relative would think to check on them, the school would remember there should be a Lizzie Fink attending classes. But inside, Lizzie would be safe. The house would make sure of it.

In the living room, she started chatting to the house again, no longer needing to be quiet and whisper into the walls. The snow fell and the house stood still, listening closely.

As Above, So Below

We learned they had arrived as most other people did – watching TV, sitting quietly before a screen listening intently to the words behind the words, straining for whatever the journalists weren't saying. A shaky image of their ship flickered on screen, just briefly, and was gone, never to be shown again. It was odd, and before the shadow of that short clip had faded from our eyes, the kids were already on their phones, scouring the internet. You'd think it would be nothing but talk of this, of them, yet it was strangely quiet. Tyler found a few tweets mentioning the evening's events, but only obliquely, no specifics. Even those, when he checked back a few minutes later, were gone.

Within a few hours, the internet was down. We thought it was something to do with our server and decided to leave it till morning. It was late anyway, and the kids had school in the morning, Mark had work. Getting everyone to bed was an ordeal. No one was remotely sleepy. The kids protested loudly and, truthfully, I couldn't see how anyone would be able to sleep. But there was no way to obtain more information until morning, and no use sitting around speculating. For a long while after everyone had been successfully tucked in bed, there was a weight to the air in the house. It was as though we could feel each other awake and breathing, even through all the closed doors. I could sense my children shifting in their beds, their strained desire to sneak into one another's rooms and discuss the night away in whispers. Mark and I said nothing, though we both lay awake for a long while. Eventually, though, we did fall asleep. The house lost its tension, its held breath at last expelled.

In the morning, of course, we found Liam asleep in Tyler's room, curled up like a cat at the foot of the bed. But Kayla was still in her room, and all three woke easily enough, no dark bags under their eyes. The internet was still down. We gathered by the TV, watching news reports that left us with little more than mounting dread. They spoke of the event of the previous night only fleetingly, and mentioned an internet wipeout that seemed to be national, perhaps even global. The vagueness of it made me uneasy, even more so when a special announcement popped up, telling us we were all to stay home today: school had been cancelled nationwide, and a stay-at-home mandate issued for the day. Under no circumstances were you to leave your house.

All day we tried to tiptoe around the nervousness. We brought out old board games, the kids dusted off an old gaming console. At some point I baked banana muffins, then cleaned the kitchen until it shone. There were books and card games and long stretches of time when we sat together in silence, each lost in some unspeakable thought.

The day passed, all the same. We were all strangely exhausted by the time night fell – from holding in all that anxiety, I think, from pretending there was nothing more happening than a strange day. We hugged each kid goodnight, even though Tyler had reached the age where parental hugs were just about the last thing he would want. I don't think we were sensing doom or anything that drastic. But there was a prevailing sense in the air that everything was about to change, and every tomorrow had suddenly become wobbly, uncertain.

In the morning, there was more of the same. The same announcement, the same lockdown. We were restless, unnerved. Mark wanted to pop to the neighbour's house, talk to someone outside our immediate bubble. But before he could even open the front door, we spotted them from the window: soldiers, marching through the streets. It was an eerie sight. My hairs stood on end; I'm sure I wasn't the only one. They weren't saying anything, or doing anything other than walking, backs straight as a rod, posture stiff. I kept waiting for someone to drive past with a megaphone, telling everyone to stay inside.

The soldiers were deterrent enough, though. Later that day we spotted Mrs Bulkin, a few doors down, trying to leave her house. There was a hulking man in camouflage blocking her way almost immediately. It lasted no more than a few seconds, then she was back inside. About half an hour later the same soldier returned, loaded with bags which we saw Mrs Bulkin accept with what seemed to us, from across the street at some distance, like gratitude.

The next morning, we woke to our own set of bags left on the front steps. Cautiously, Mark and I went to fetch them. A few neighbours were doing the same, with identical packages. We waved awkwardly, aware we were being watched. I wondered if every street had sentries now, and how could they possibly manage that? How were they organising it? The soldiers weren't there continuously, we'd noticed already, but frequently enough, with no discernible pattern, to still be dissuasive. At first, I had thought they were there for our protection, that we were being kept inside because something had not gone well with our visitors from far, far away. But bringing the bags in, feeling the entire neighbourhood teem with apprehension, I wondered.

The bags were filled with groceries. To be honest, the thought of food hadn't crossed my mind yet – we had stocked pantries, plenty to last a while anyway, partly a result of Mark's childhood of deprivation. The strangest thing was how accurately the bags had been filled: basics like meat and rice and a slew of vegetables, but also Kayla's favourite raspberry Jaffa cakes, the household's standard coffee brand, the chocolate chips I always had on hand for baking, Liam's favourite fruit juice. I don't think the kids noticed the strangeness – not the youngest, anyway – but Mark and I exchanged a loaded look while we put things away. I knew he was as disturbed as I was.

We hadn't been talking about it, as strange as that may sound. I think we were both scared, and scared for our kids most of all, and it was difficult to face the situation. I think we were waiting for the powers that be to resolve this, and for life to return to normal. We could talk about it then, about how strange it had all been. Once the danger had passed. Yet on day three of being locked in, it seemed increasingly less likely that things would resolve easily. We did sneak upstairs then, close our bedroom door softly, only to stare at each other for a long moment, unsure how to word all our fears, the situation so outside our control there was little we could plan for. Yet we could see all of that in each other's eyes. We were in perfect harmony – I do remember the bitter-sweetness of it that came over me later, of feeling so closely linked, so absolutely understood, but over something so dark that it stole our words. We spoke a different language, with hands and mouths and extraordinarily delicate love, hurried and frantic, aware of the children downstairs.

A week passed like this, in a haze. It's odd how quietly we fell into the new routine, how little we questioned it. Only once did we catch a glimpse of someone trying to leave their house, causing a bit of a scene, shouting at soldiers. Someone whose name we hadn't learned yet, newly moved into the neighbourhood. He'd made it to the middle of the road before the soldiers got to him. We couldn't hear what he shouted, but nonetheless we had the kids move away from the windows, despite their protests. Both Mark and I were afraid we were about to witness violence, guns gleaming in the autumn sun, indistinct movement and red spilling on the pavement. None of that happened, though. The soldiers, a handful of them surrounding the escapee, talked to him in calm tones, despite the man's yelling. They took hold of his arms and marched him home. Their movements weren't cruel, though, or harsh in any way. They seemed to carry him off almost gently. I caught a glimpse of Mark's face as we watched this, his eyes wide in amazement. I'm sure I looked much the same.

I don't know why we weren't more upset at the state of things, frankly. We were lucky – we had a backyard, and it was not yet cold enough to make it unpleasant. The broadcasts were vague, told you to not leave your house, but the soldiers only patrolled the streets and our yard was fenced in all around, blocking anyone's view. It was a risk, perhaps, but one we took nonetheless. Sometimes I would catch myself breathing in deeply, looking for something in the air, a scent or a sense, something to justify our quarantine, something to say we were fools for not sticking to the mandate and sneaking outside. But I could detect nothing, and the soldiers walked around freely enough, no masks on.

It was late one evening, after the kids had gone to bed, that Mark and I sneaked out and sat on the back porch step, looking at the stars. I don't know if it had been a frequent occurrence or if we just happened to look up the one time it happened. Either way, the sky was full of lights, far in the distance, up high enough that we couldn't tell – were they in the sky or in space? Had we ever considered that boundary before? I assuredly had not, though I had learned, along with everyone else, the names of the layers in our atmosphere, now long forgotten. Somewhere in there, or up higher, it was impossible to tell, the lights hovered and moved. Half a dozen, at least, brighter than the stars. At first it was hard to tell which way they moved, but as we sat and watched, it became clearer they were coming in, down. They moved much slower than I expected. How many were there now? How many such arrivals had we missed, stuck indoors? How many all over the world?

Mark and I sat in silence, staring up long after they were gone from the sky. By the time we went in I had a crick in my neck, an aching pain that spread to my shoulders when we got into bed. Neither of us could sleep for a long while, yet we didn't talk about that either. I reached for Mark's hand in the darkness and turned my back to the bedroom window. I didn't want to see, even through the closed blinds, so much as a flickering of light.

A few days later they let us out again. It was so unexpected that we sat in front of the TV trying to process information long after they announced we were free to leave. The broadcast was more or less the same as it had been the whole time – the same backdrop, the same newscaster stringing words together in a way that makes it seem as though they're saying a lot while actually saying very little. Freedom beckoned and still we sat, transfixed. Then a knock on the door came, loud, a shotgun breaking our frozen silence. Tyler got to the door first, before Mark and I had time to advise caution. A redhead girl stood there, nervous energy emanating from her in waves. She was a blur, throwing herself into Tyler's arms the moment he opened the door. He caught her and held on. I glanced at Mark but he looked more amused than anything else.

'Is it okay if I head out?' Tyler asked us, when the embrace finally ended. He did not look at us, but kept his eyes on the girl.

Mark shrugged, though Tyler couldn't see it. 'Stay close,' was all he said, and the two of them were out the door in a flash.

'Did you know about that?' I asked Mark in the shocked stillness of their departure. Mark only shook his head and got up, heading outside too. It broke the spell and we all spilled out onto the sidewalk together. Liam held Mark's hand tightly and Kayla stayed close to me. All over the street the scene was the same: families emerging looking dazed, glancing around as though afraid a soldier was about to come and usher them back inside. We drifted easily to the neighbours closest to us, the Mallick family, with whom we'd shared many a summer barbecue. In a surreal string of events, they invited us for dinner and we gathered in their home and cooked together, as though it was merely a normal Tuesday. The kids played in the living room while we cooked, assisting Reva in making a sort of impromptu feast. We talked about things only obliquely, in hushed tones, exchanging loaded glances. It was as if the temporary lockdown had been a blanket over us and we were all now afraid of speaking above a whisper, lest we get caught, like misbehaving children, and get grounded again.

It was a relief, though, to be with them again. We ate and laughed and shared a bottle of wine. And if we glanced outside repeatedly, scanning the streets for threats we could not name, no one commented on it. The TV stayed on, though we could barely hear it from the dining room as we ate. We were all, I think, feeling a great mixture of things, not least of which was a low hum of anxiety for whatever came next. We were prisoners, granted a brief surprise release, sure of our inevitable return behind bars.

We returned home early, despite the desire to linger longer. We were all wary, and I wanted to be home when Tyler returned; the worry for him had kept half my brain occupied the whole evening. The sun had yet to set – though we had called the meal 'dinner', it had been at an odd time, and night had not yet started to gather around us. Tyler, thankfully, joined us as we were making our way home. Much as I wanted to ask him about the girl, I kept quiet, aware of the fragility of the situation, of his need for privacy, especially in such strange times.

It was a few more days before the internet came back on. Those were the oddest of times, I think. Nobody knew quite what to do and there didn't seem to be any good way to find out. The majority of our jobs couldn't be done without the internet, especially not after a long break. The corner shop opened first, the baker's the morning after. Gradually things returned to a new sort of normal. When the internet returned, the relief was immense. Yet it still took time to figure things out. There had been a clear chain of command when everything had come to a screeching halt, a sense that someone was in charge and knew what they were doing. But the aftermath was much more confusing, as businesses tried to restart operations and even most government branches seemed to be stumbling about in the dark. It wasn't until we were online again that we realised how lucky we'd been, in our little street. We'd had food and shelter and our basic needs met. I hadn't thought much, truthfully, of others who hadn't fared as well. Stories about medical emergencies gone unanswered, riots violently suppressed, whole towns without electricity for the week. It was chaos, and it was hard, impossible, to listen to it all, take it all in.

Yet from the noise, something emerged, inevitably. Videos, taken from windows of apartments by the sea, dark and grainy, mostly, but still clear enough: their ships, giant shapes in the darkness, a few lights on, pointing nowhere in particular, floating above the water. Moving out and under, sinking slowly under the waves. In some of the videos you can hear the reactions of the people filming, the shock and fear in their voices, the confusion; others are totally silent. But in some you just hear the ocean through an open window, the displaced waves, the sound of the ships as they settle on the surface and break it, drop below it. And the after, once the ships are gone from view and everything looks much the same, the waves crashing more restlessly for a few heartbeats before settling to their constant, ancient rhythm.

Those are the scariest videos. We had to watch them a few times to figure out why they were so unsettling, more so than the rest. It was the quiet of the ships themselves. They made no sound as they moved. You could only hear the ocean as it greeted them and accepted them and continued its song.

There was no official word, really. Some half-hearted attempt at suppressing the videos and the chatter they created. Some vague nothings from a few world leaders. But afterwards life resumed, shockingly. There were uproars, of course. Demands for information. A million podcast episodes on the subject. Wild theories thrown left and right. But though there had to be a significant group of people who knew what had happened, who had helped orchestrate something, no one was cracking. There were no information leaks, only speculation. It's hard to keep a fire going when there's no fuel.

A few brave or inane souls tried to make an investigation of their own. Boats and divers making excursions out to sea, looking for answers. Some found nothing. But quite a few disappeared beneath the waves as well, dove down and never resurfaced. There was a steady stream of those, for a while. It's outstanding how many humans think they'll be the exception. Then again, I'd say a fair amount of them knew they wouldn't come back from whatever was out there, they just couldn't not know, the curiosity was eating at them, a parasite stealing all their energy.

We settled back into life. Tyler brought the redhead home; Nell loved my homemade cookies and was a champion at ping-pong. Mrs Bulkin moved away, we saw her get picked up by her son and his family, waved goodbye as the car turned the corner and vanished. Her house stayed empty for a while, but eventually a new family moved in. It was strange to think of these strangers – people who had not gone through the same thing we had, but had their own version of events, had their own stories we knew nothing about. I wondered if all over the world people were bonding over this, over a sense of shared experience that was so universal yet so different from neighbourhood to neighbourhood.

Things did go back to normal, though. Time keeps passing and we had to move with it, I suppose. But people moved away from coastal towns. No one wanted a beach vacation anymore. Sometimes there would be a set of strange news reports: sharks washing up dead on the shores of Australia, whale song caught on tape in new tones, which to our human ears sounded eerie and lost. Fishing boats gone missing, rogue waves surging, massive walls of water hitting the shore unexpectedly. We learned to leave the sea alone.

We still watch the stars, sometimes. Kayla has found a new love of astrology, mapped our entire family according to maps only she understands. In warm evenings we sit outside, fire up the barbecue, invite the Mallicks over. We look up, occasionally. Kayla pointed out Cetus, once, the whale. I followed her finger as she connected the stars above us, but frankly, I couldn't see it. Perhaps I didn't want to.

It is silly to say, to think it, but the world feels heavier. I keep thinking about the displaced water, when they sank. Like when you sit in the bath and the water rises around you. Where did it go, that water? I'm sure there are smarter people than me out there, trying to figure it out. I avoid baths now, anyway. I can never stop my head from dipping under the water, and every time I do, I swear, I can hear the ocean, pressing all around me.

Riverquick, Saltfresh

I was ten when I found a fragment of a seashell – a perfect pearly pink, with etched ridges equally spaced. Its edges had been rounded by the sea. Something about it really called to me. The colour, I suppose, most likely – it was such a sweet, soft shade of pink, one I'd never seen or associated with the ocean or any ocean-dwelling thing. Finding it, half buried in the sand, felt like a gift to me personally. From the sea itself.

This was a week, give or take, after my sister died. Everyone too broken up about that to really notice or care that I'd wandered off down to the beach. The sound of the waves was so soothing to me, probably because no matter how loud they got it was still quieter than home, now filled with constant wails, screams, sometimes even the occasional plate thrown against the wall. I'm sure I didn't quite grasp the accusations my parents were throwing at each other, back and forth like a corrupted tennis ball, a sick game of hot potato with an emotional bomb always just about ready to go off.

It was my fault, of course, not theirs. But they didn't know that and there was no need to tell them.

I kept the seashell on me for weeks, in a pocket where I'd have easy access to it and could hold it whenever things got too much. Rubbing the raised surface with my thumb, back and forth, back and forth, became like a comfort reflex. Long after the shell was gone I'd find myself repeating the motion, caressing nothing more than a half-remembered shape. But after I found it, I held on to it as though it was my lifeline, the one thing anchoring me to safety, keeping me from drifting in the water the way Esther had. I found myself at the beach time and time again, as though keeping watch, waiting for her to rise from the waves, wash ashore and walk home as though nothing had happened. This is where she would be, I knew. The river would've spit her out to sea, and I kept waiting for the sea to spit her back out – she was ours, after all; she belonged to us land dwellers.

She never did, of course. They never found her body. Though Mum would see her face in every seal, like she wanted to believe her daughter had not fallen in the river after all but had taken up a selkie skin instead, and slipped away to a new life.

She would have, too, is the thing. If she could've, she would have.

For a time, I was certain that it was mermaids who had delivered the seashell to me, made sure I could find it on that beach. Still young enough to dream of long wavy hair and shiny green scales, pink conches for breasts. Little mermaid dreams, hoping for magic that was suddenly all gone from my world. For a time, I was hoping for mermaids because it was easier than hoping for Esther, and often I couldn't tell which would be more realistic, which had a higher chance of happening. When someone finally noticed that I kept disappearing for long stretches of time, I was confined to my bedroom for days. This was the thing to finally unite my parents, for a time anyway – their anger now turned towards me, poisonous in its sharpness, my mother shouting that I was trying to kill her, that she'd been through enough, that she'd be damned if the water was going to take anything else away from her. It's easy to see now how the grief broke her in so many different ways, but back then all I knew was the corrosive power of her words, the sound of a key in the lock, keeping me in, and the loss of my potential mermaid rescuers.

But time passed and their anger turned away again, towards themselves and each other, and possibly the whole world. Either way, their focus shifted and they forgot about me once more. I felt a kind of relief at that, there was something bittersweet in being freed from my captivity. My parents wouldn't hold me anymore, I suppose because I looked too much like the daughter they'd never get to hold again, so in a strange way being locked in a room felt like their arms around me, half protective and warm, half suffocating and restrictive. But in my room it was hard to picture Esther, not even looking in the mirror to see such an exact smaller replica of her standing there with eager eyes. To picture her now, I needed the sea: the smell of seaweed, the layer of salt crusting over my skin. I should've played it safe, maybe, but it was where I first went when I was once again allowed out – to the sea, to walk the endless beach, scouring the sand for any washed-up mermaids.

I can't say even now, with the power of hindsight, what was true from the beginning and what was projection, desperate hope tangled with desperate fear turning the edges of reality around me just a wee bit bendier than normal. I do remember walking barefoot, shoes clutched to my chest so I wouldn't accidentally drop them in the water, with the sea lapping at my feet, feeling distinctly like the water was pulling me, tugging at my feet, trying to drag me in, that it would've succeeded if only I moved just an inch closer, just an inch deeper. Feeling the tendrils of fear climb up my legs and spread around my body. The idea of a sentient North Sea seemed somehow so terrifying as to make everything else matter just a little less so. Perhaps it crossed my mind that this was where my sister now lived, in the belly of the sea, being digested by this massive monster, being unmade. In truth, I am not even sure if, when I first heard the voices, they were really voices at all, and not the caws of the seagulls distorted in my mind until it sounded like words. I couldn't decipher what they said, the first few dozen times, only went home and dreamt of Esther, draped in an ocean-blue ballgown that fell to the floor in waves, fabric shimmering at her feet like foam, beckoning to me, asking me if I, too, didn't want to wear the sea like a party dress.

I did not try to resist the call from the depths. I kept seeing the day she died, the park all but deserted, her swimsuit the same blue-grey as the river, her laughter as she dipped her toes in the water before floating away. She laughed, for a moment she was all laughter, overflowing with the joy of being one with the water. She must have felt the current change beneath her, though, grip her tighter, because she started flailing and she screamed my name, once, sharp, quickly swallowed by the river. I feel like I can still see her eyes, frightened, but she was too far away for that, it all happened so quickly. In no time her head was beneath the water and I could see her no longer.

I knew where the river led, I had learned that much, so I was sure she would pop out like a cork at the end of the river, flow into the sea and meet me at home. Yet when a mother pushing a stroller came into view on the path, I pretended to be playing, throwing pebbles into the river. I waited until she was gone to run home. I told myself Esther would come crawling out of the sea, but I still lay awake in bed, sweating, I still told no one what I had seen.

I think I knew for sure she wasn't coming back when I watched grief take my parents like the tide, pulling them away to where I could never reach them again. Each day that passed drove them further out until I felt like an island, alone.

So when the sea sang to me, of course I gave in. That was the easy part.

My sister wasn't there, when I made it underwater, half expecting a greeting party. There was no sign of her, neither of her dancing with the waves nor of her rotting body sunken in the sand. There were no castles made of gleaming shells, no crowned white-haired merman come to welcome me. When I reached in my coat pocket for my pink seashell – a reflex I wouldn't grow out of for years, even though there would be nothing there to find – it was gone. Lost somewhere along the sand above, or lost in the mists of the sea, snatched by a passing wave, who knows. Part of me had believed that shell was a glimpse into this underwater world, a dazzling shade of pink, perfect symmetry, soft edges. Sea magic, children's stories of the Disney-tinted variety.

Nothing at all like the hands that found me and pulled me under, with hungry eyes and sharp teeth. It was so dark at the bottom of the sea, so dark and so cold. Esther had been a summer child, made ecstatic by water rafting and wild camping, craving adventure with such a free heart, eyes always wide open so as not to miss anything. She wouldn't have enjoyed this, the cold so deep it was a hand around your throat. I was glad, then, that she wasn't there. I hoped she had floated further away, maybe gone sea-hopping until she found the right one for her, the Mediterranean, maybe, or the Red Sea, the saltiest sea with all its beautiful reefs. I hoped she was there and not stuck somewhere here where the water is so frigid it sometimes hurts to dip your toes, even in the summer. Esther deserved warm waters, if anyone did.

Not me, clearly. The North Sea, and the things within it, were all I would get. I endured it as they swam around me, watching me with those dark eyes, reaching out a webbed hand to touch my skin. They felt soft, not slimy as I'd imagined, like they were made of velvet. One had held my hand all the way here, to the bottom of the sea, my feet slipping in the wet sand beneath, rocks digging into my soles, fish darting away when they saw us coming. We walked past a jellyfish the size of my head, and I was scared, for a moment, more scared of that translucent being than of the grey creature pulling me along. We moved past the jellyfish with no incident, though. The sea is so big, it can hold so much. There is room.

I couldn't hear the voices anymore. I don't know when I started wondering whether I had imagined them at all, or whether they had been the ghosts of the drowned warning me away, trying to hold my hand too and pull me in the opposite direction, except they were too insubstantial. Or perhaps down here the ocean filled my ears too much to allow for words to wiggle in. They circled me, silently, in the dark, taking turns reaching out and feeling me, as though this was their language, their hellos. One stood behind me and gathered my floating hair. I imagined it braided intricately, decorated with seashells. I imagined brightness into this dark place. Instead, I watched it float away from me as they cut it, dark tendrils little more than shadows in the water. I had not felt the need to breathe under here yet, but as they approached me, these salt-drenched things from the deep, I felt a pressure on my chest, like my lungs waking up. I tried to hold it as long as I could, but their hands covered me and I took a deep breath.

I have found bones at the bottom of the sea, so many bones. Some have writing on them, like promises for an afterlife that never came. None of them are Esther's; I know, I checked. I licked each one of them clean to see if I could taste her. I was so sure that the river would've carried her to sea. I have walked all the way to Norway and back, to no avail. Esther is not here, though I do not know whether I planned to join her or bring her back if I had found her. I do not know if I meant to apologise for watching her splash into the water and disappear beneath it without saying a thing. Perhaps that is why I had to do my own version of the same. Perhaps she is, indeed, floating beneath the Red Sea, surrounded by her own version of mer-people.

I think of leaving, sometimes. Of swimming to the surface and tracking salt water all the way home, telling my mum I was the one taken by the selkies. But then I feel the sea, hugging me all around. It's such a tight embrace, how could I ever leave it. How could I ever leave these loving arms.

The Wall

I t was Sunday evening and a light rain had just begun to fall. It was so light you could barely hear it hit the windows. The house was silent, except for the groan of old wood settling and the creaking of pipes to serve as background noise. Anne-Marie stood at the foot of the stairs. The flickering light from the fireplace danced across the polished floorboards as darkness gathered outside.

'What is it?' Lars asked from his seat in the living room. Though he was close enough, his voice echoed slightly. *Carpets*, Anne-Marie thought, not for the first time, *we should get some more carpets.*

'Nothing,' she said, still not moving. 'I thought I heard something, that's all.'

There was no reply from Lars. He was an outline in the darkness.

'How about a cup of tea?' Anne-Marie asked, stepping away from the staircase only to stand uncertainly in the hallway, the house seeming to stretch too large around her. It was an uncomfortable sensation she had never gotten used to, that the house was too large a container for so small a filling.

Lars grunted in response. Anne-Marie knew him well enough now, after so many years of marriage, to recognise the meaning behind it. She went to the kitchen, hearing the shuffle of her house slippers against the wooden floor.

'We should get a grandfather clock for this hallway,' she said, raising her voice as she moved away. In the silence of the house she thought it unlikely that Lars could fail to hear her, whatever volume she used, but still, it was more his attention she needed to capture first.

'Hmm?' she heard in response, and nothing more. Shaking her head, she made them both tea, carefully setting everything on a doily-lined tray and arranging biscuits on a small plate. There was no need for it, she well knew, for the artifice of formality, but it was Sunday and today she felt, more than normal, that curious pulsing absence in the house.

Lars was focused on his book, a philosophy treatise on morality he was struggling to get through; the author was dull and never seemed to make his point clearly, only circle around it as if approaching skittery prey. The small print was giving him a headache, though it was not until Anne-Marie turned on the lamp beside the armchair that it occurred to him he had been reading mostly in the dark. She set the tray down with a sigh and sat, leaving the tea to steep a bit longer. She fidgeted in her seat, eyes glued to the dancing flames. Lars sensed within her that old restlessness, but tonight he did not have the patience or the heart to indulge it. He reached the end of his paragraph, set his book down, and poured them tea.

The Wall

They drank in silence for a while. If there was an allotted number of words a couple could exchange in one lifetime, they were far from reaching their limit – yet most of the time they coexisted in silence as though afraid they would reach it at any moment. It was not necessarily a comfortable silence, most of the times, but an almost irritating one.

'Did you mention a grandfather clock?' Lars said, breaking the stillness.

Anne-Marie turned to him and he could see that her cheeks were flushed from the warmth of the fire. 'Yes,' she said. 'For the hallway.'

'What for?'

'I think I would like to hear it tick,' she said. They lapsed into silence again, sipping their tea. Lars reached over and patted his wife's hand, before picking his book up again. Anne-Marie stared at the flames and listened to their crackle.

Theirs was a townhouse in an affluent part of the city, on a tree-lined street where cars were parked neatly and rubbish never littered the pavements. They made a pretty picture, all the houses lined up, in red brick with white trimming, and beautiful bay windows that sparkled in the sunlight – always the glass panes shone, kept so clean you would think no rain or speck of dirt ever fell upon them.

Inside, the wood floors were polished to perfection and no dust was permitted to linger. Anne-Marie woke early every morning, before the sun had risen, and went around the house quietly dusting, adjusting things minutely to her liking, wiping the kitchen counters anew, despite having done so before going to bed. Then she went from window to window and drew the curtains, just as the sky was lightening. It was a ritual awakening for the house and she liked to see it neat, to stand by her kitchen window and drink her morning coffee looking out into the back garden, where overgrown bushes and flowers had been allowed to grow wild. By the time Lars made his way downstairs, she would often be on her second coffee, drinking it outside if the weather was good, sitting on an old garden chair while the birds twittered in the trees. The garden was secluded, high fences surrounding it on all sides for perfect privacy, but to Anne-Marie it was the plethora of sounds she treasured most, the illusion that, despite how contained she was within it, she still belonged to the world and all its human noises.

Lars never went out into the garden. The sight of it repulsed him, overgrown and unkempt as it was, though he would never dream of doing anything to fix it. He liked to stay by the fireplace, as much as possible, and disliked summer and its overbearing heat, the way it made the very air around seem thicker and forced them to keep windows open. Through the cracks (for he never liked them opened any wider than a crack) he could hear the cars in the street, and it was impossible not to picture the exhaust fumes making their way inside, polluting his home.

Inside was quiet, indeed, but it was a quiet he could see the shape of and, sometimes, managed to find some comfort in. Still, perhaps he would get that grandfather clock his wife wanted.

Late evening the next day, on an ordinary Monday, the couple were getting ready for bed. Lars stood by the bathroom sink and brushed his teeth while Anne-Marie laid out an outfit for the next day. She worked part-time three days a week as a secretary for a local charity organisation, and liked her morning routine to be particularly sharp those days. Lars had somewhat less to worry about – he was an accountant and wore a variation on the same suit and shirt every day. It required little to no thought to assemble his outfit each morning, and his wife took care of everything else: by the time he made his way downstairs each morning the breakfast table would be set, coffee brewing, toast toasting, his lunch made and carefully wrapped up ready to go.

Both were preoccupied, thinking of the week ahead, when they first heard the crying. It was high pitched and decidedly unpleasant, clearly a baby continuously screeching as loudly as possible. Startled, both froze: Lars with toothpaste dripping onto the sink and Anne-Marie holding a pencil skirt in the exact shade of turquoise blue to match her favourite earrings. As the baby kept crying, Lars spat out his toothpaste and peeked from the bathroom to find Anne-Marie's eyes. As they looked at each other, the sound seemed to swell around them and fill the room.

'A baby,' said Lars, needlessly.

'So it would seem,' his wife replied. She moved towards the wall and placed her hand there, as though she could feel the vibrations from the infant's cry resonating through the house itself.

'Quite the set of lungs,' Lars said, and Anne-Marie nodded absent-mindedly. Lars, after a moment, resumed preparing for bed. Anne-Marie stood a while longer, her hand on the wall, listening. The crying stopped abruptly just as Lars was getting into bed, and the two of them shared a look, heavy with meaning, and said no more on the matter.

'It must be Mrs O'Brien,' Anne-Marie said, buttering her morning toast. There were shadows under her eyes though she had done her best to disguise them with makeup. She had had a restless night, waiting to hear the baby's cry resume. There had been nothing, though, and try as she might, she couldn't hear the smallest sound of life from next door – no footsteps, no coughing, no gentle humming to calm a newborn.

'I hardly think Mrs O'Brien could cry quite at that pitch, dear.'

Anne-Marie shot her husband a look and refilled her cup of coffee. 'Really, Lars.'

'I thought there was no Mr O'Brien anymore,' he said.

'There isn't. You should know, you attended his funeral.' Again they shared a look. It had been much too long since an outside event had rekindled this between them, the loaded looks, the casual intimacy of knowing one another well enough that words become redundant.

'Well,' Lars said, and they both fell quiet again before Anne-Marie noticed they were, in fact, running late, and hurried them both along, leaving the dishes in the sink. *A few minutes of crying and already this baby is causing a disruption*, thought Anne-Marie. Still, she felt a kind of delicious shiver run down her spine as she ran out her front door and glanced towards her neighbour's house.

That night the baby, half-forgotten by both, woke them with its cries. The noise of it was immense, a ridiculous volume, as though the baby was not next door but right there with them. Anne-Marie sat up straight, the duvet falling away from her. Immediately she was cold, her skin breaking into goose pimples. In the darkness of the night, with the cold enveloping her and the cries of the baby filling up all available space, a sense of unreality swept over her. Lars was slower to react, and in that interval Anne-Marie felt herself momentarily adrift in a kind of nightmare.

'What time is it?' asked Lars, sitting up himself. The slimmest hint of light shone through a gap in the curtains, not shut carefully enough, and Anne-Marie thought it must be a full moon night.

She got out of bed without replying, fitting her feet into her slippers and wrapping her robe tightly around her waist.

'Where are you going?'

'I don't know, I can't just lie there.'

'But what are you going to do?'

Anne-Marie felt as though they were shouting to be heard over the noise. 'I'll go and make a tea,' she said, 'you can't possibly think anyone could sleep through that.'

Anne-Marie swept out of the room and headed downstairs in the dark. In the kitchen the sound was slightly muffled, and Anne-Marie felt strangely grateful, fearing, without realising it, some more ominous crying than that of a regular baby. Was it normal for a baby to cry like that? She could not remember. She heard Lars coming down the stairs and set to making tea for two.

Lars was not old, but he felt, just then, like grumbling

his way down the stairs and maybe pounding the wall in annoyance. Still, if the baby was this loud on their side of the wall, how unbearable must it be even closer. He felt some sympathy for the mother, though he could hear no evidence of anyone but the baby on the other side. The cries were simply too overwhelming.

He lit the small lamp in the living room and knelt to make a fire. The house was cold, the floor beneath his knees frigid. The fire was slow to catch, mostly because his hands would not stop shivering. By the time he had stoked the flames to his satisfaction, Anne-Marie was there, carrying a tray with tea and biscuits. They sat on their armchairs and sipped their tea, the symphony that had gotten them out of bed still ringing through the house.

They both wondered, to themselves, if they should be doing something more proactive. Heading over to Mrs O'Brien's house to offer help, or make sure nothing had happened, calling someone – but who? They did not bring it up, and as the room warmed up around them they both drifted, eventually, back to sleep in their chairs.

In the morning, it was quiet again. Lars and Anne-Marie set about their day as usual, each carrying an extra load of exhaustion.

When he left work, Lars took a detour to an antique shop close by his bank. He had walked past it for years and had always seen, somewhat in the back but visible from the doorway, an old grandfather clock. He wasn't thinking of the noise, god knew they'd had enough of that now, but of his wife and the look on her face when he came home with it. He didn't give himself much time to think it over, just bought it and had the delivery arranged. It was made of beautiful oakwood and Lars knew it would look perfect in their hallway.

He was right. That evening, when the clock was delivered and arranged just so, Anne-Marie stood and admired it with girlish glee. The clock was taller than her, dark, polished and ornate. She fell in love with it immediately, couldn't wait for the first time it chimed – she clapped her hands when it did, standing before it excitedly.

Lars laughed. 'Wait till it wakes you in the night,' he said. They both fell quiet at that, reminded of the alarm clock that woke them the night before. *Perhaps*, Lars thought, *this was a mistake.*

For a few days an unsteady routine formed: the baby would cry, at all hours of the night, and they would get up and head downstairs. The clock was forgotten; they barely noticed it chime anymore. A night or two later Lars fell asleep in his armchair and never even made it to bed; Anne-Marie slept uneasily without him next to her but was too reluctant to wake him, not when sleep had become so precious. Some nights were quiet, but they both woke anyway, an inner clock keeping them alert, in suspense, waiting. Lars kept expecting they would get used to it and sleep through the racket, but they never did. They never heard anything else, no sounds of a mother pacing to pacify a colicky baby, or singing it to sleep, or even a second set of tears, which would have been understandable given the unrelenting nature of the baby's own. The screaming baby was much too loud for any other sound to leak through, perhaps.

After a week of this, nerves fraying at the edges, Anne-Marie finally decided it was time to visit Mrs O'Brien. She baked a batch of cinnamon muffins – she had, in fact, forgotten how much she enjoyed baking and how it filled the house with the most delicious fragrance – and set them prettily into a basket, like she was Red Riding Hood heading to her granny's house. She left Lars poring over his book and crossed over to the neighbour's front door. Mrs O'Brien's front yard was tidy, but Anne-Marie noticed the first small signs of neglect: weeds starting to grow on the planters next to her rosebushes, limescale showing at the bottom of the wall. It was to be expected, she supposed, that such things wouldn't be priority with a newborn around.

She knocked decisively and waited, as the sun started to make its slow descent towards evening. When Mrs O'Brien finally came to the door, she looked like a lost girl. Anne-Marie struggled to think of her as Mrs O'Brien, though she knew that she had married and been widowed quite young. She and Lars had attended Mr O'Brien's funeral a couple of years back, despite having had so little contact with their neighbours. Lars had spoken to the man a few times, he had said he seemed a good man. The funeral had been sad and so sparsely attended that Anne-Marie felt gratified they had gone after all.

What he would say now to seeing his young bride with a baby, she could not say.

'Oh,' Mrs O'Brien said, in a small voice. Her hair was messily tied into a bun and seemed unwashed for quite some time. There was a large stain on the front of her dress, the faded red of strawberry jam. 'Mrs Andersen,' she said, sounding a little alarmed. She opened her mouth as though to speak again but seemed to hesitate, unsure of what to say. Anne-Marie smiled, she hoped kindly, and extended the basket. 'I brought you some muffins,' she said, and Mrs O'Brien smiled back at her, weakly, before opening the door wider to let her in.

Mrs O'Brien's house was somewhat in disarray. The living room, where she led Anne-Marie, was covered in a fine layer of dust, and there were unopened packs of diapers and baby toys in a corner. She set down the basket of muffins on a table and offered her guest some tea, barely giving Anne-Marie time to agree before she fled the room. Anne-Marie listened but heard no signs of a baby. She sat down on the leather couch and waited patiently.

The room was furnished quite plainly, with the exception of a tiger statue in a corner, a few feet high and pure white. There seemed to be no dust on it, but Mrs O'Brien had not thought to turn on a light and the sunlight was rapidly vanishing. The fireplace was not lit but the heating was clearly on, as the house was warm, almost stuffy. In the corner of the couch was a folded knitted blanket and Anne-Marie had a vision of Mrs O'Brien folding it around herself and stretching out on the couch once the baby was asleep, one hand extended to pet the tiger.

She returned with a tray carrying tea for two and plates. She handed a muffin to Anne-Marie before sloppily pouring tea into their mugs. Anne-Marie thanked her and set her plate down, watching as Mrs O'Brien took a big bite of her muffin. For a few moments Mrs O'Brien focused solely on her muffin, while Anne-Marie sipped her tea. The teacup was chipped, she noticed, and carefully rotated it so she wouldn't cut her lip. She wished she had brought a casserole instead, or a large pot of soup. She tried not to notice the crumbs falling on the floor.

'These are delicious,' Mrs O'Brien said, mouth half full.

'I'm glad.'

When she had finished with her muffin, she glanced at Anne-Marie and set her plate down carefully, brushing crumbs from the corner of her mouth. She cleared her throat.

Anne-Marie, now that she was here, didn't quite know what to say to this girl, barely twenty by the looks of her, clearly tired and only just holding herself together. What had she come to say, really? Had she come to complain of the noise? It seemed ridiculous now, in the gloomy room, sitting next to her fragile neighbour, that she could say anything at all.

'Does your family live nearby?' Anne-Marie asked, figuring there was no need for polite preamble. Mrs O'Brien shook her head. She seemed to finally realise how dark the room had become and got up to turn on the light. The harshness of it, glaringly bright all of a sudden, hurt Anne-Marie's eyes. She longed for her own living room with its soft lighting and perpetually lit fireplace.

'I would be more than happy to look after the baby if you need someone, you know,' she said, before knowing she would say it. She could not snatch the words back, though they swelled in the room, uninvited. She couldn't imagine coming here, to this house, to care for this baby, nor could she picture it in her own home. She thought she could feel Lars through the wall, suddenly raising his head from his book, a disapproving frown aimed at her.

'That's very kind of you,' said Mrs O'Brien. 'We're just getting settled in, you see.'

'How old is it?'

'Just three weeks.'

Three weeks was, surely, an absurd age for any being to be. Mrs O'Brien must have seen some shock on Anne-Marie's face for she smiled, very slightly, and poured herself more tea.

'I am sorry about the noise,' she said, and so they had arrived, quite suddenly, at the crux of the matter. Anne-Marie made a sweeping gesture, as though dismissing the subject entirely. In the bright light she could see Mrs O'Brien's dark circles, thick under her eyes. She got up, abruptly, a suffocating claustrophobia coming over her. Startled, Mrs O'Brien rose as well.

'You just call on us if you ever need anything, will you?' Anne-Marie said, already heading out of the room.

'Thank you, Mrs Andersen, it was very kind of you to drop by,' Mrs O'Brien said, rushing to keep up with her. At the door Anne-Marie paused and let her host open it. She squeezed her hand once, quickly, before disappearing down the steps and crossing into her own home. She did not look back to see a confused Mrs O'Brien standing alone in her doorway.

Lars had read the same sentence several times that evening. He had no desire to go visit the neighbour, but at the same time he could not deny an intense wish to know what the two women were talking about. If only their voices would carry as loudly as the baby's did. He tended to the fire, stoked the flames higher, and forced himself to sit down with the book again and not pace the room.

When his wife came through the front door, looking harried, he stopped himself from rising in his seat to meet her and waited for her to come to him instead. She stood at the living room doorway for a moment, hands clutched together, and Lars noticed, perhaps for the first time, that his wife had grown old. Not very old, no – but older, the fine lines around her eyes more pronounced than he remembered, her blond hair a duller colour, lying flatter against her head. She had a slight hunch, standing there in her green dress, and a lost look that filled him with tenderness; but a distant tenderness, one tinged with sadness, with the knowledge of having looked upon your loved one and seen a stranger superimposed with the person you thought you knew.

'I can't bear to think of that girl, all alone with a baby, in that big house,' she finally said, and it seemed to break her paralysis. She walked in and sat on her armchair, without bothering to take off her coat. 'I know the man is dead, but to marry that girl so young and bring her here, and then to have the audacity to die and leave her entirely alone!'

'Well,' Lars said, and fell quiet again. He reached out and patted her hand, but she looked too far away to feel it.

'I'm making tea,' she announced, and got up once again. Lars was sick of tea, but he let her go without a word. In the hallway, the clock chimed and he flinched, as though the sound was brand new.

That night, again, the crying. Lars woke to the sound and found his wife was already out of bed. He saw a splinter of light from the bathroom and heard her crying, such a soft sound, almost lost in the cacophony of the baby. He blinked in the dark and turned over, decided he'd try to get back to sleep where he was.

He lasted two minutes before angrily getting out of bed and marching downstairs.

They stood by the spare bedroom and considered it. It was almost empty, just a bed and a nightstand and a small chest of drawers in one corner. The room was cold and had a slight damp dusty smell from being closed up for so long. Anne-Marie thought of the wallpaper they had bought for this room, so many years ago, now rotting in the attic, and quickly shoved the memory away.

'It's still too close,' Lars said. They both turned and faced the far wall, still only a small hallway and set of stairs away. He sighed. 'At least we wouldn't be sharing a wall,' he said.

Anne-Marie nodded, shivered, and went to open the windows in the room. Then she closed the door, not wanting to see more of the room than she had to just then. After they had eaten dinner and night had fallen, she returned and closed the windows, the room frigid now but the smell mostly gone, and turned down the bedding before changing her mind and stripping the bed entirely and fetching fresh sheets to put on. Every sound echoed, the room too large and bare and with no softness in it to absorb sound.

When they went to bed, Lars dragged a lamp over from another part of the house and set it on the one nightstand. He plugged it in, set his book next to it, determined to be lulled to sleep in this new environment. Anne-Marie shivered next to him as she got into bed, the sheets cold from the cupboard. If only she had thought to warm it with a hot water bottle first. Still, after some tossing and turning, she seemed to fall asleep, the even rise and fall of her breath a comforting sound that allowed him to relax into his book.

A chapter later, the baby started crying.

Anne-Marie woke immediately, as she always did. She looked around, disoriented, and Lars reached out to try to comfort her. Visibly alarmed, she recoiled from him and nearly fell off the bed. In a moment, she realised where they were and fled downstairs. Lars half-expected to look around and find a ghost waiting to chase her. He followed her more sedately, noting, with overwhelming disappointment, that the closed door and the extra space between them and the baby seemed to do very little to dampen the sound. A piercing headache emerged when he was going down the stairs, and though they both drank cup after cup of tea, neither managed to fall asleep in their armchair until morning.

The baby cries. He is loud, his screaming piercing the night like a knife. They are shocked that no one has complained, that other neighbours' sleep isn't disrupted like theirs. Every night Anne-Marie thinks she will go back to visit Mrs O'Brien, every morning she feels incapable of doing so, feels as if they have gotten too old and have never really had to care for a baby and so don't realise this is just how babies are.

Some nights are so bad the two of them make up scenarios in hushed tones: Mrs O'Brien, naked, drawing a pentagram on her floorboards with chalk, doing something unspeakable to the baby – cutting him, just a little each night, drinking a bit of his blood, or pouring it into a chalice as an offering to a satanic god. Things they could never say in the daylight, that they never, in fact, acknowledge having said at all. It's just that the baby is so loud, producing sounds so unnatural, that they can only think, in the night, that either the baby is being tortured or is, itself, the torturer, a demon baby of some kind, driving them all insane.

When the baby cries during the day, it somehow doesn't seem quite so unsettling. It is still loud beyond comprehension, still brushing against unbearable, but there is a film of normality over it: outside cars drive by, the postman stops to deliver some mail, Anne-Marie hoovers the stairs when it starts to wail and is thankful for the extra noise to cover it. On the weekends, Lars lies down for an afternoon nap after another night awake, only to have the baby interrupt that too. He nearly punches the wall, his despair curling inside him into a deep bitterness.

Exhaustion settles over them like dust, accumulating a new layer each night. Anne-Marie's pity and sympathy for Mrs O'Brien curdles. She no longer thinks of the empty crib they once had to force themselves to throw away, of a room boarded up and ignored, with the same pang of sorrow she cannot let herself feel. She is divided: part of her wants to hold that baby and soothe it to sleep. She knows it would work – she knows if she rocked it gently it would settle down and look up at her with absolute trust and drift into peaceful slumber.

Another part of her wants to take that baby and bash its small fragile skull against the wall until it is finally quiet.

It was inevitable, really. Lars returned home from work one morning incensed. He had fallen asleep at his desk and his boss had caught him. It was a miracle and a mercy that he wasn't fired on the spot, and that only because his long years of good service vouched for him. The dressing down he got pressed itself under his skin; the situation had reached unmanageability.

He slammed the door behind him when he came home and Anne-Marie, stirring a pot of soup in the kitchen, jumped. Lars came to find her, his anger seeping out into the air around him.

'I cannot take this anymore,' he said. He did not want to explain to Anne-Marie why today had been the last straw. She looked startled, and a little afraid. They were both jumpy these days, strung out. Anne-Marie had begun to obsessively check that she had, in fact, turned off the oven every evening. Now she turned to him and let the soup bubble behind her untended.

'This is unacceptable,' he said. 'We are both losing our goddamn minds!'

Anne-Marie fought the instinct to tell him to lower his voice lest the neighbour hear. The irony brought a bubble of laughter to her throat, and she realised there was an edge of hysteria to her now. She found herself nodding along.

'We have to do something,' Lars was saying.

'That baby is clearly being neglected.'

He stopped and pointed at her, triumphantly. 'Yes! Yes it is! This is not natural!'

'I offered to watch him for her, I offered help,' she said, while behind her the soup bubbled over the pot.

'And she didn't take it! She could've had help! Truly this is too much!' His words were punctuated by his righteous fury; he was strangely energised, pulsing with emotion.

Anne-Marie was already undoing her apron, folding it neatly, still nodding along. 'We've been so patient.'

'No one would have been as patient as we have been!'

And together they moved as one, out of the kitchen and towards the entryway. Halfway down the hallway, Anne-Marie remembered the soup and turned back to turn off the stovetop. The soup was surely stuck to the bottom now, the pot ruined, the stovetop dirty and already crusting as the spills dried. She left everything as it was and joined Lars once again. Together, they marched outside and across to their neighbour's front door.

When Lars knocked on Mrs O'Brien's front door, he did it forcefully, three strong knocks that would be heard through the whole building. In their haste, they had left the house as they were: Lars wearing his business suit and his over-coat, Anne-Marie in her dress, a slight cardigan over it but no coat. As they stood on the doorstep, snow started to fall gently, the first of the season. Neither noticed; Anne-Marie wasn't even cold.

Mrs O'Brien came to the door, looking much as she had when Anne-Marie had last visited, though perhaps a bit more dishevelled. Her expression, upon seeing them, was not inviting. She looked not just worn down, but fraying at the edges. She, too, appeared about to break.

'I'm so sorry but now is not a good time,' she said, already closing the door. Lars did not miss a beat and blocked her attempt with his foot. Mrs O'Brien looked at him and said nothing more.

'We just want to talk,' he said, and Anne-Marie wanted to laugh at the cliché.

'Please,' Mrs O'Brien said, much too weakly and much too late, as Lars was already forcing his way inside the house. Anne-Marie followed him and closed the door gently. She did not stop to pay attention to what Lars was saying to Mrs O'Brien as he held her against the wall, she simply moved past them and up the stairs, to where she knew the baby must be. When she reached the top of the stairs, the baby started crying, like it wanted her to find him – it knew, he knew, that rescue was coming. She rushed to the door at the end of the hallway, the house mirroring hers so closely that she felt slightly disoriented.

In the crib, the baby looked up at her, face red and tear-stained, mouth wide mid-scream. But when he saw her, the crying ceased abruptly. Anne-Marie's ears rang in the silence, her heart swelled. The baby's eyes, wide, an eerie shade of blue, much too bright, stared up at her in wonder. She felt tears well up in her own eyes and pictured them both crying together – not the scream-crying he'd been doing, but regular crying, the kind easily soothed by a mother's love. She reached down to pick him up and his skin was hot, his legs bare, a diaper peeking out from his beige bodysuit, covered in little tigers. He had the slightest wisp of hair on his head, a light shade of brown. Anne-Marie kissed the top of his head and the baby was still and absolutely quiet as he took her in.

Lars would have loved an excuse to lash out, even at someone as small and helpless as Mrs O'Brien. With his arm crossed over her collarbone, pressing her into the wall, he was closer to her than he had ever been. It made him realise he had never really noticed her before. She was much younger than he thought, her skin still flawless, though a pasty white now and too dry from the cold. Her lips were chapped and bitten; even as he watched, she gnawed on a corner until she drew blood. She looked scared and tired and so young. It brought to mind someone else, now long gone. How old would *she* have been now? But no, no, the ages didn't line up, there was no reason to think it.

Mrs O'Brien was crying, her tears an endless stream, her eyes so bloodshot he wondered if she had been crying for days. Lars looked around, uncertain about his purpose now. The house was a mess, clothes and toys strewn everywhere. Surely the baby was too young for toys? Through the open living room door, Lars saw the basket of muffins Anne-Marie had brought, what looked like one mouldy muffin left inside. In the corner, a fallen statue, broken in pieces on the floor. Lars could not tell what it had once been.

They heard the baby start crying, and, shortly after, stop.

'He won't stop crying,' Mrs O'Brien said, tears clogging her voice. 'No matter what I do, he won't stop crying, I can't make him stop. I've taken him to several doctors, there's nothing wrong with him, they say there's nothing wrong with him, but he won't stop.'

Lars opened his mouth to reply, but found he had nothing to say. He pressed her harder against the wall, but she did not react. There was no satisfaction in attacking someone already so obviously broken.

'He won't stop,' she was saying, over and over again. 'He won't stop, I can't make him stop.'

When Anne-Marie came down the stairs carrying the baby, Mrs O'Brien's crying intensified. She was sobbing now, would have doubled over from the weight of her tears if Lars hadn't been holding her up.

Anne-Marie came close to them and looked at Mrs O'Brien, a strange beatific expression on her face. 'We will take care of him,' she told their neighbour. 'I promise.'

Mrs O'Brien, to Lars's shock, nodded and collapsed against the wall, her legs no longer able to hold her up. Lars scrambled to keep her upright and eventually just lowered her gently to the ground as his wife stepped around them and headed to the door. Mrs O'Brien did not look up to watch them go, only covered her eyes and rested her face against her drawn-up knees, still sobbing.

'You'll be okay,' Lars told her, awkwardly caressing her hair. 'Get some rest now.'

Before he left too, he could've sworn she said thank you.

Anne-Marie sent Lars out for essentials: diapers, baby formula, baby powder. She couldn't recall, exactly, everything a baby needed, but she was sure they could figure it out, they could get through the night and make a better list tomorrow. Outside, it was snowing more heavily. She had covered the baby as much as she could as she crossed the yard back to her house, but snow had still fallen upon his skin. He had not cried, though, only watched in wide-eyed wonder as the snowflakes fell all around.

Inside, she sat with him by the fireplace, unwilling to set him down for a moment. When Lars returned, she would send him up to the attic. She was sure she had saved some things, a baby blanket at least, perhaps a pacifier. Was he too young for pacifiers?

The Wall

'We will figure it out together, don't you worry,' she whispered to the baby. She realised just then that she had never learned his name. It didn't feel important, anyway. She rocked back and forth slightly and wished for a rocking chair. Another thing to add to the list.

The baby was still quiet, transfixed by her face. He kept his little hands still against his chest, but Anne-Marie was sure that soon they would want to explore and touch her skin. She could not wait for that moment.

That night the baby slept peacefully, the whole night through. So did the Andersens. They had improvised a cot of sorts, out of a cardboard box and blankets, so the baby could sleep in their bedroom. For a while they had both stayed awake, checking the baby eagerly, anxiously, waiting for it to cry. Anne-Marie had made up a bottle of baby formula, but the baby had not seemed to want it, so they let it be, trusted that he would tell them when he was hungry. They had heard his strong lungs before, after all.

Eventually, exhaustion stole over them, though. They slept through the night and well into the morning. Around eleven, Lars woke up, groggy and mildly confused, and called his office, told them he was sick and could not come in. Anne-Marie was not working that day, so Lars let her sleep a little longer as she had no one to call. He watched her, face slack in sleep, mouth slightly open. She looked gaunt, her skin had a grey tinge to it that he knew was brought on by their long stint of sleep deprivation. He checked on the baby, who was awake and staring silently at the ceiling.

Gingerly, cautiously, he picked up the baby. He looked perfect, with round puffy cheeks and that little wisp of hair. He took the baby downstairs and made a mess of changing his diaper. He figured it out in the end, and was exhilarated, felt like whistling in his joy.

Outside the world was blanketed in snow. When Anne-Marie woke, he would go check on Mrs O'Brien, he decided.

But when Anne-Marie woke and took the baby, Lars opened their front door to find a couple of bags left on their doorstep. They were dusted with snow, but Lars could still see the footprints that led from Mrs O'Brien's house to theirs and then made their way out, down the street. He brought the bags in, found a diaper bag and diapers, as well as a plastic bag filled with baby clothes, diaper cream, baby wipes, baby bottles, thermometer. A million little things they had not thought of yet. Lars stood by the window and looked out at the footsteps again. A heaviness set over him. There was no note with the baby things.

The second night the baby slept peacefully again. They were filled with elation, a sense of peace, of righteousness. Clearly the baby was happy now. Clearly they had done the right thing.

On the third night, the baby woke them, screaming so loud that Lars fell out of bed in alarm. Anne-Marie reached the baby first and picked him up, though the sound emanating from him was so loud she wanted to cover her ears – or maybe the baby's mouth. She thought her eardrums would explode. But no amount of rocking would calm the baby down. His diaper did not need changing, he refused the bottle. They sang to him, they rocked him, they paced with him, they even took him outside, into the back garden, just for a moment, thinking the shock of the cold might give him pause, the sight of the snow falling might fill him with wonder once again.

Well into the morning he cried. His little voice was so piercing they both felt sure it would deafen them soon, and what a relief that would be.

When the sun rose, the baby finally quieted down. Anne-Marie wept in relief. Lars left, trudged through the snow to knock on Mrs O'Brien's door. But no one was home. He'd already known that, but had needed to be out of the house anyway. When he returned his wife was calmly feeding the baby, and he lay down for a nap. They would get through it.

On the fourth night the baby woke again. He howled. The sound would have ripped your heart out of your chest, if you hadn't been so busy checking your ears weren't bleeding. It was a good thing, they supposed, that the house to their left had been empty for years. At least they were sandwiched between empty spaces now, no one left to bother.

Though Anne-Marie was the one holding the baby, Lars felt he could not take it another moment. He went outside, stood in the snow for a long while, looking up at the bright starry sky. He wanted to cry, but was too exhausted. He looked over at Mrs O'Brien's house once again, before returning to the warmth of his home.

He found his wife sitting by the fireplace, on the floor, rocking back and forth with the baby in her arms. He could see her lips moving, but had to get quite close before he could make out what she was saying over the din.

'It's okay, baby,' she was saying, her tone reassuring, like she was trying to convince the baby. 'You're okay. You're safe now, you're safe. Safe as houses. Safe as houses, baby.'

In the hallway, the grandfather clock chimed, but neither of them could hear it.

Acknowledgements

About the Author

About Dead Ink

Dead Ink is a publisher of bold new fiction based in Liverpool. We're an Arts Council England National Portfolio Organisation.

If you would like to keep up to date with what we're up to, check out our website and join our mailing list.

www.deadinkbooks.com | @deadinkbooks